Best Wishes

Jeanne Packer
12/8/12

Olive

A Fictional Account of the Life of Olive Ann Oatman

Jeanne Packer

authorHOUSE®

AuthorHouse™
1663 Liberty Drive
Bloomington, IN 47403
www.authorhouse.com
Phone: 1-800-839-8640

First published by AuthorHouse 8/4/2010

ISBN: 978-1-4520-1468-5 (e)
ISBN: 978-1-4520-1466-1 (sc)
ISBN: 978-1-4520-1467-8 (hc)

Library of Congress Control Number: 2010906687

Printed in the United States of America
Bloomington, Indiana

This book is printed on acid-free paper.

ACKNOWLEDGMENTS

Kathleen Yetman, for her diligence in tracking down most of the images in this novel

Kate Reeve, Arizona Historical Society, Tucson

Rebekah Tabah, Arizona Historical Foundation, Tempe

Mina Parish, University of Arizona Library, Tucson

Pat Foley, Mohave County Museum, Kingman, Arizona

Susan Snyder, Bancroft Library, Berkeley, California

Dorothy Kupcha Leland, author of *Sallie Fox: The Story of a Pioneer Girl,* for information about the Rose-Baley wagon train incident on August 30, 1858

Greg Michno, author of *A Fate Worse than Death,* for his encouragement and assistance with source material

Matt Lawrence, my coordinator at Author House, for his expert guidance

Cyndy Muscatel, my writing instructor, who urged me to write with clarity and incisiveness

Alida Pask, Smithsonian, American Art Musuem

Darla Wingren-Mason, Smithsonian Institute Libraries

Theresa Erickson of Oatman, Arizona, my dear friend who took me to the Needles Museum and the Mohave Museum in search of material for my book

Pearl Gray, my good Canadian friend, who slashed my first chapter unmercifully and set me on the right literary path

Cindy Lee, my cleaning lady and friend, who read my manuscript and gave it a rave review

ACKNOWLEDGEMENTS

This book is dedicated to my husband, Harry, who put up with late dinners and a wife who seemed to be joined at the hip with her computer. This is also dedicated to a new generation of readers who will, hopefully, be inspired by the sacrifices of the pioneers who unified this great country.

PREFACE

This fictionalized version of the life of Olive Ann Oatman did not spring unbidden from my imagination; rather, it evolved from my obsession with the main character. From the moment a co-worker loaned me a copy of Lillian Schlissel's *Women's Diaries of the Westward Journey,* and I saw a photograph of Olive Oatman, complete with tattooed chin, I was hooked. I was determined to learn all I could about her. I traveled all over the state of Arizona, garnering information from museums, libraries, and anyone who would talk to me. After accumulating several books, a few old magazines, and two file drawers of notes, I began to organize everything and started writing.

Much has been written about Olive Oatman, but always in narrative style. I wanted her to come alive, and I hope I've succeeded. Rather than "the virgin captive among the savages," as she has heretofore been portrayed, I wanted to deliver her to the reader as a flesh and blood woman forced to accept unspeakable hardships and life-shattering choices that take their toll on her once-indomitable spirit. Olive survives, though not without cost.

Olive Ann Oatman, 1857

Prologue

The body of Joseph Smith, founder and leader of the Church of Latter-Day Saints, dangled at the end of a sturdy rope tied securely to the branch of an old oak tree. He had been incarcerated in the local jail in Carthage "for his own protection" against the angry citizens of Illinois who had become incensed by his inflammatory rhetoric. He had openly advocated polygamy (plural marriage) and arranged marriages between older men and very young girls. He publicly proclaimed that "all religions (except Mormonism) were an abomination." He wrote the Book of Mormon, claiming an angel named Maroni had appeared to him and revealed the truths contained in the book. He claimed to have the ability to locate lost items by placing "seer stones" in a hat and "reading" them.

The rapid growth of Mormonism alarmed the good people of Illinois, and Joseph Smith began to receive death threats. One of Smith's followers had managed to smuggle a pistol into the jail in anticipation of trouble. Everything came to a head on June 27, 1844. That night, an angry mob attacked the jail. Smith shot three of his attackers, killing two and wounding a third. Joseph's brother Hiram was killed in the skirmish. The vigilantes abducted Joseph Smith, and, when they had ridden a safe distance from town, they hanged him.

The warning was clear. Mormons were not welcome in Illinois. Following the death of Joseph Smith, Brigham Young became the new head of the Church of Latter-Day Saints. He embraced all of the teachings of Joseph Smith, particularly plural marriage. Young threatened to excommunicate anyone who failed to practice polygamy. He organized a mass exodus of Mormons out of Nauvoo, Illinois, in February of 1846 to found the "Promised Land" where they could practice the tenets of their religion free from interference. Approximately five hundred in number, they would become known as the Mormon Battalion. Their quest would end at the Great Salt Lake in Utah.

Others remained in Illinois and broke off into splinter groups with various new names to disguise their Mormon origins. One such group was the Brewsterites, led by James Colin Brewster, a charismatic man in his early forties. He stood about six feet tall and possessed a spare, ascetic build, dark, penetrating, deep-set eyes, and a full, black beard. He was ambivalent about plural marriage. He neither condoned nor condemned it.

Chapter I
Fulton, Illinois

On a chilly, windswept Sunday in late April of 1850, Olive Ann Oatman sat poised on the edge of a hay bale in the barn that served as a temporary church. She was thirteen years old, and her life was about to change forever.

Sitting there flanked by her parents and six siblings, she could not have imagined the cruel fate that life had in store for her and her family.

Now, the entire congregation leaned forward in anticipation. Not a sound could be heard. Even the barn swallows that flitted among the rafters were silent.

Olive looked expectantly at James Brewster as he stood on a rough platform at the front of the barn and raised his arms above his head. He seemed to wait until he was sure all eyes were fastened on him. Then, in a booming voice, he made the announcement everyone had been waiting for: "At last, we are ready to pursue our vision of the promised land of Bashan."

He paused dramatically. Assured that he had their rapt attention, he continued, "On the first Monday in May, we will meet here, at the church. We will bow our heads and ask the Lord to bless our journey and protect us from harm. Then, at nine o'clock, we will depart from this place and proceed to Independence, Missouri. There we will meet up with other Brewsterites and join the wagon train that will ultimately take us across the mighty plains through the wilderness to the promised land of Bashan, where the mighty Colorado River flows into the Gulf of Mexico.

"Now, go to your homes and farms to make final preparations. Gather your loved ones and neighbors. Say goodbye, and ask them to pray for your safe and successful journey. I will see you here on Monday morning. If you are not here and prepared to leave by nine, we will go without you. This will be the practice for the duration of the journey. Rules must be established and strictly enforced. This is necessary for the good of the entire group. Until Monday, go in peace. The Lord be with you. Amen."

The congregation echoed his "amen" and filed out into the small churchyard. The wind whipped about them, tossing men's hats into the air and women's skirts billowing about their legs.

Olive stood in the churchyard, waiting for her father and brother to bring the wagon around. She clutched at her bonnet and attempted to hold her skirts down with her free hand while the wind assaulted her unmercifully. She turned slightly in an effort to deflect the wind and, in so doing, found herself looking into the laughing eyes of Robert Kelly. She was momentarily distracted; just long enough for a sudden gust of wind to lift her skirt and petticoat in a great balloon which revealed more of her legs than was deemed proper for a modest young lady. She blushed and laughed as she fought to gain control of her wayward skirts. Robert laughed out loud.

Robert Kelly, a carpenter by trade and an Irishman by birth, was born on the Isle of Man on December 25, 1825. He was twenty-four years old, six feet tall, and well-muscled from hard physical labor. His auburn hair was shoulder-length and held back by a strip of rawhide fastened at the back of his neck. He had mischievous, dark blue eyes that bespoke his Irish heritage. He was clearly attracted to Olive.

The Oatman wagon pulled up sharply in the churchyard, sending dust and pebbles into the swirling air. Olive helped her younger siblings into the waiting wagon and, stepping onto the side rail, she vaulted cleanly over the side, landing squarely on the hard board seat next to little Mary Ann. She stole a sideways glance at Robert. He was still laughing, and now his older brother, John, was laughing too.

"Isn't she the lively lass?" Robert exclaimed.

John turned to Robert. "Isn't she a bit young for you, Robert?"

"Not at all. Mormon girls marry young, and most marry older men. Besides, take a look at her, John. She's a full-grown woman."

Olive looked over at her big sister, Lucy, who was sitting next to Mary Ann.

"I guess they enjoyed my flying leap into the wagon." She laughed.

"I missed it," said Lucy, smiling. "I just hope you didn't show them your bloomers." They doubled up with laughter.

"Olie, I'm cold," Mary Ann whimpered.

Olive looked down at her little sister. Mary Ann was the personification of an angel. Her blonde ringlets escaped from the little woolen hat framing her delicate features and cornflower-blue eyes. Olive hugged her close.

"Hush, baby, I'll warm you," she said. Then, with a mischievous grin, she turned her head to the side and caught Robert staring at her. Her long, dark hair blew about her face in wild abandon. Her eyes were the color of topaz, startling against her smooth, white skin. She was fun-loving and given to spontaneous laughter. At school, she was known for her intelligence and sense of humor.

Royce Oatman cracked the whip smartly, and the two-horse team leapt forward and trotted out of the churchyard.

Mrs. Oatman sat beside him on the buckboard, holding eighteen-month-old Roland on her lap. C. A., age three, sat between his mother and father. Lorenzo, fourteen, alternated between walking alongside the wagon and riding on the rear bumper. Lucy, sixteen, rode in the wagon with Olive, thirteen, and Mary Ann, seven. Lucy kept a tight grip on Royce, Jr., age five, a spirited child with a talent for trouble.

The Oatman family was nine in number, seven children and their parents, Royce and Mary Ann. In the summer of 1849, when he heard about Brewster's plan to lead his followers to the "Promised Land" at the confluence of the Gila and Colorado Rivers in the New Mexico territory, Royce Oatman decided to join them. He sent his application and fee to James Brewster, and the Oatman family became regular attendees at the Sunday services in the makeshift church in Fulton.

When they reached the farm, Lorenzo unhitched the horses and led them to the barn, where he groomed and fed them. Then he went into the house, where the family was preparing for Sunday dinner. Everyone, except the baby, had their duties, and it wasn't long before they were all seated at the table.

Mr. Oatman lowered his head, folded his hands, and began to pray.

"Thank you, Lord, for your bounty which we are about to receive. Amen."

The children echoed, "Amen."

They proceeded to tuck into a hearty meal of cornbread, sausage, and home-canned carrots.

The children asked questions about the journey ahead.

"Will there be Indians?"

"What will we do if there are Indians?"

"Will everybody have guns?"

And from fourteen-year-old Lorenzo, "Will *I* have a gun?"

Royce Oatman answered their questions patiently, and, after the table had been cleared, they adjourned to the living room.

Soon, friends and fellow travelers began to arrive, and a lively discussion followed. Taking part were Mr. and Mrs. Ira Thompson; the Kelly brothers, John and Robert; Dr. and Mrs. Lane; and Mr. and Mrs. Willard Wilder. Their conversation revolved around the long westward journey and what provisions would be required. They discussed guns, ammunition, food, and supplies. They exchanged ideas regarding the necessary livestock, horses, oxen, milk cows, and mules they would need for the trip.

While the grown-ups discussed these important matters, the children sat in a circle, listening to Bible stories, which Olive and Lucy took turns reading. Now and then, Olive would steal a glance at Robert Kelly as he conversed with the men. She admired his strong profile and how he became animated during the discussion. Lucy noticed her preoccupation.

"Olive, will you stop staring at Robert? It's your turn to read."

"I'm sorry. I was just thinking that he's a grown man and I'm still a child."

"You're old enough to marry, Olive. I've seen how Robert looks at you. I only wish a man would look at me that way. I'm sixteen and practically an old maid."

4

They laughed, and Olive picked up the storybook and began to read aloud again.

At eight o'clock, the visitors said their goodbyes and climbed into their wagons for the long ride home. Robert lingered at the front door, holding his hat. Then he nodded toward Olive. "Night, Miss Olive," he said, smiling devilishly. He put his hat on and walked to the fencepost, unhitched his horse, and mounted it. She stood in the doorway, watching Robert and John ride toward the highway and vanish into the cool, starry night.

Chapter II
A Fresh Start

It was no secret that the last two years had been a disaster. Royce Oatman had been plagued with poor health. He had a back injury and a chronic respiratory problem that was aggravated by the cold Illinois winters. He was a medium-sized man, about five and a half feet tall, with black hair, a round face, and a full, black beard. From his boyhood, he had been given to recklessness, with a wanderlust and love of adventure. He had attended schools in western New York until he was about nineteen years of age. He then became anxious to head west to the prairies of Illinois.

His parents, Lyman and Lucy Oatman, had been running a hotel in Layharp, Illinois, for almost a year when Royce joined them. There he met and married eighteen-year-old Miss Mary Ann Sperry of Layharp. Second to the eldest in a family of nine children, she was intelligent and learned quickly. Therefore, she was better educated than most young women of that era. She and her family had moved to Layharp from the east coast, where she had been educated. Though she was not beautiful, she was possessed of a very sweet nature. She was sedate, affectionate and very religious.

The first two years of their marriage were spent on a farm near Layharp. Royce Oatman opened a mercantile business in town, and prosperity followed. The country filled rapidly, and farmers were becoming rich as the standard of living improved. Paper money became plentiful, and many people invested beyond their means in real estate improvements.

The banks chartered from1832 to1840 had issued money beyond their charters. There was a severe reversal in the local economy in 1842. Produce was a glut on the market, and many long-standing debts became due. When the banks failed, Royce Oatman found himself several thousands in debt and completely insolvent.

He had relatives in the Cumberland Valley of Pennsylvania, and within three months, he departed with his wife and family of five children to seek his fortune in the Cumberland Valley. After three disappointing months in Pennsylvania, he moved his family to Chicago, where he secured a teaching position. They remained in Chicago for one year until, in the spring of 1846, they traveled to Fulton, Illinois, staked out a claim, and began farming. After he sustained his back injury, Royce found it more and more difficult to keep up with the demands of a farm.

Once the decision had been made to join the fifty-two Brewsterites of the Colorado River Camp, Royce Oatman made plans to raise the necessary capital for the westward journey. In the spring of 1850, he sold the farm for $1500. He used the money to purchase an outfit consisting of three yoke of oxen, two milk cows, and three riding horses, plus enough provisions for eighteen months of prairie and desert travel.

Their farm wagon was transformed into a Conestoga by the addition of rounded metal staves and canvas stretched over them to provide shelter in all weather conditions. In a compartment beneath the wagon's floor were stores of jerked meat, dried berries and apples, flour, corned beef, cornmeal, preserved fruits and vegetables, bacon, and beans. Also stored below were bedding and clothing.

Olive and Lucy had worked far into the night with their mother, their needles flashing in the light of the oil lamp, in their rush to complete their clothing requirements. Each girl would have two calico dresses for warm weather, and one linsey-woolsey dress for cooler days. The dresses were loose-fitting, long-sleeved, and high-necked. They stopped just short of the tops of their sturdy lace-up boots. A calico sun-bonnet completed the outfit. The male members of the family wore trousers of a sturdy, tight-woven, twill fabric in a dark color. They each had three light weight shirts and one warm linsey-woolsey shirt. Sturdy lace-up boots and a hat completed the outfit. All family members had warm cloaks fashioned from wool blankets.

Olive and Lucy soon discovered that tying an apron about the waist gave their figures definition, despite the shapeless cut of their dresses. As an added bonus, aprons also served to protect their dresses and carry miscellaneous items.

Chapter III
The Journey Begins

It was with a mixture of excitement and a pang of regret at leaving all that was familiar and dear to them that the Oatman family set out for Independence, Missouri, on the first Monday in May, 1850. As the wagon pulled out of the yard and onto the road, little Mary Ann, her eyes brimming with tears, turned to Olive.

"Oh, Olive, I will miss my swing."

Olive turned and looked back at the forlorn little swing suspended from a branch of the old apple tree in front of the farmhouse. She felt a chill and a heavy sadness, but for Mary Ann's sake, she shook it off.

"Don't worry, dear. You'll have another swing when we reach Bashan. Father says it's sunny and warm there, even in winter, so you can swing all year 'round."

Mary Ann brightened, snuggled against Olive, and soon fell into a peaceful sleep.

They had gotten a late start, and Royce Oatman decided to head straight to the main road instead of going to the church to meet the others. He planned to make up the lost time and catch up with the other wagons along the way.

At the outset, the sky was overcast as the wagon bumped along over sodden roads. It had rained the night before, and every leaf and blade of grass was sprinkled with heavy dew. The children walked and skipped alongside the wagon, happy to be on the move at last, their restless sleep of the previous night forgotten with the promise of adventure.

Now and then, they passed a farmhouse, and people came out to wave goodbye and wish them well. Along this road, the farmers had become accustomed to seeing covered wagons heading toward Independence to join the great wagon trains that would take them west. Many enterprising villagers approached the wagons with homegrown produce, poultry, fresh-baked bread, and pies to tempt the travelers and supplement their own meager incomes.

They had gone about thirty miles when they heard their mother scream. The wagon ground to a halt, and their father leapt from his seat and ran to the side of the wagon. C. A., age three, lay under the wagon, just behind the wheel that had run over his neck. He had been sitting on the front seat between his mother and father when the wagon hit a bump. C. A. was ejected and thrown under the wagon. Royce Oatman knelt beside the limp body of his little son and gently picked him up. Cradling the unconscious child in his arms, he walked to the side of the road, where he sat, praying over the boy. Mother sat down beside them, holding her baby, and began praying with him. The other children gathered around and sang hymns

After what seemed an eternity, C. A.'s eyelids fluttered, and he began to cough. There was a bright red bruise on his neck where the wheel had passed over it, but he seemed otherwise unharmed. They placed little C. A. inside the wagon on a soft mattress, and, with Lucy watching over him, the family moved on toward Independence.

The following letter was written by Royce Oatman to a friend on July 30, 1850, from Independence, Missouri.

> I left Fulton City on the first Monday in May, for Bashan, the land of peace, with my family, nine in number. About thirty miles from there, my little boy, about three and a half years old, fell out of the wagon, and the wheel ran over his neck. I took him up and saw that he was about to depart this life. Not feeling willing to part with him, I administered to the child according to the law and order of the gospel, and the Lord blessed him. He soon recovered and is now hearty and well.

This incident made a powerful impression on the children. They were convinced they had witnessed a miracle and that prayer would protect them, no matter what dangers lay ahead. They would soon learn that there were times when prayer was not enough.

Chapter IV
Wagons Ho!

Ira Thompson and family joined the Oatmans at Muscatine, Iowa. Besides Mr. and Mrs. Thompson, there were two daughters: Susan, seventeen, and Lucy, five. Susan Thompson and Lucy Oatman had become good friends after meeting at church several months ago. They hugged each other and laughed, delighted to be traveling together. It took a month to travel through southern Iowa and northern Missouri.

When the Oatmans and the Thompsons arrived in Independence, Missouri, they sought out their friends amid the hustle and bustle of the busy town. They managed to complete their last-minute purchases and made preparations for their departure. The town was flooded with people heading to California to prospect for gold. The Mexican-American war[1] had lasted only a year, from 1846 to 1847, and California was now a territory of the United States. With the discovery of gold at Sutter's Mill in Coloma, California, in January of 1848, hundreds of people were heading west to seek their fortunes.

An experienced wagon master walked among the wagons, inspecting their loads and admonishing those who had brought household furnishings and other heavy items that would be of no use to them on the long westward journey.

"Get rid of some of that stuff, or you'll break an axle in the middle of the desert. You'll get stuck in the mud when you try to cross a river.

---

[1] The Mexican-American War began on May 13, 1846 and ended one year later. The treaty of Guadalupe Hidalgo was signed on February 2, 1948 giving the U.S. control of Texas, establishing the Rio Grande River as the U.S.-Mexican border, and ceding to the U.S. the present day states of California, Nevada, Utah and parts of Arizona, New Mexico, Colorado and Wyoming. Mexico received $15,000,000 in compensation and the U.S. government agreed to assume $3.25 million in debt owed by the Mexican government to U.S. citizens. Many Americans had opposed the war from the start. Among the opponents was General Ulysses S. Grant who, in his memoirs published in 1885, condemned it as an "unjust war." Mexico had lost 500,000 square miles, or 40%, of its territory.

You'll overturn when you hit a rut," he shouted, loud enough to be heard over the din.

A flourishing business called "offloading" had sprung up in Independence. These entrepreneurs walked among the wagons and offered ridiculously low prices to the emigrants for their possessions, knowing they had no choice. More often than not, scavengers offered to simply cart their goods away without remuneration. It was heartbreaking to see people in tears as they watched their family heirlooms being hauled away by these land pirates.

At last, after several delays, they were ready to begin. The command was given: "Wagons ho-o-o!"

Excited cheers mingled with the cracking of whips, the creaking of wheels, neighing of horses, lowing of oxen and cattle, and the jingling of cowbells. Pots and pans, dangling from hooks on the wagons, clanged and banged, contributing to the general din.

Most of the wagons were drawn by three yoke of oxen, and a few had teams of horses. The children ran and skipped alongside the wagon train, happy to be moving at last. The entire Colorado River Camp, consisting of fifty-two Brewsterites in twenty covered wagons, finally departed Independence, Missouri, on August 9, 1850.

It was decided that they would convene at Council Grove, Kansas, about a hundred miles from Independence on the old Santa Fe Road, away from the noise and crowds of the town. For a while, everything was congenial. They planned to travel about fifteen miles a day to prevent the livestock from becoming exhausted. The evenings were festive occasions, with everyone gathered about the campfire to sing hymns and recite prayers.

New friends were made and old acquaintances renewed. The children regarded it as one big picnic. Lucy, the eldest of the Oatman children, helped her mother with cooking and caring for the baby and C. A., while Olive kept an eye on Royce Jr. and Mary Ann.

During the week at Council Grove, James Brewster held many meetings, during which he laid down rules for the group. He selected his friend, Jackson Goodale, as leader of the Colorado River Camp.

Royce Oatman was anxious to get underway. He considered the week at Council Grove a total waste of time. As the week came to an end, friction and grumbling became more and more prevalent within the ranks of the Brewsterites. Olive would later recall that "all dissension was due to the peculiarities in religious penchants of certain restless spirits in our company."

As they passed through the occasional towns and scattered farms of Kansas, people came out to greet them and wish them well. As the last of the farms faded from sight, the wagon train entered upon the vast, unknown region known as "The West."

Chapter V
Young Love and "Injuns"

They had been on their way only a few months when Mary Lane, a young girl of nineteen, died of tuberculosis. She had been sick when they started, but her uncle, a physician who was also part of the wagon train, had hoped that the outdoor life would cure her.

There was no timber available on the prairie, so each family gave a board from their wagon for the casket. When they left the grave on a little hillside at dusk and heard the howling of the wolves drawing nearer, they were beset by a so-called "terror of the plains." The mood around the campfire that night was somber and morose as they mourned the loss of Mary Lane and pondered the tenuous nature of their own mortality.

The weather was perfect, with cool, invigorating evenings, a much needed respite from the day's heat. Peace was restored and all sources of irritation forgotten as the party moved on to the Big Bend of the Arkansas River.

Every two or three days, a stop was made, and while the women baked and washed, the men hunted for antelope, buffalo or smaller game such as rabbits and pheasants. Often, when camped near a stream, fresh fish supplemented their diet.

Each morning, after they had milked their cows, the women would tie a churn of cream to one of the cross beams supporting the canvas top of the wagon. In the evening, when they halted for the day, they had fresh butter for their biscuits. The jostling of the wagons did all churning.

In the evenings, they gathered about the campfire and played games, told stories, or danced. Susan Thompson played the violin while the travelers sang, danced, and shouted out their requests.

"Play 'Money Musk,' Susan" or "Let's hear 'Zip Coon,' Susan."

Susan was always happy to oblige, and the young folks would skip out into the circle around the campfire and dance a jig or a Virginia reel.

On one of these festive occasions, Olive was dancing with her older sister, Lucy, when Robert Kelly stepped into the circle, took her hand, and whirled her around and around until they staggered into the tall grass, laughing and gasping for breath. They fell, exhausted, on the soft, fragrant blades, and Robert said, "I'm glad I came. John talked me into it. We're not Brewsterites, you know. We heard about the Brewster wagon train and decided to go along for the companionship."

"I'm glad you did. There's safety in numbers, especially if they can shoot as well as you and John. I watched your target practice yesterday."

"You did, eh? John and I like to hunt. It's good practice for pickin' off Injuns. Hope we don't have to, but it's best to be prepared."

"Well, I certainly feel much safer having you and John with us."

"That wouldn't be a bit o' your blarney now, would it?"

She laughed. "Whatever do you mean, Robert? You know I'm a good Christian. I never lie but I might stoop to flattery, if that's what you mean by 'blarney.'"

"That's close enough. I'll have to teach you to speak Irish. But first you'll have to teach me to dance." He laughed. "I was sure I'd have a good time on this trip as soon as I heard you were going."

Olive blushed. "Now, that's pure blarney if I ever heard it." They both laughed. Robert took her hand and held it.

The music had stopped. Susan was putting her violin away in its case, and people were heading for their wagons. Olive and Robert reluctantly stood up and brushed themselves off. They said their goodnights and headed toward their wagons.

Later that night, despite the gaiety of the evening, Olive overheard two men arguing about their differing religious beliefs.

Why can't everyone just get along? Our faith should unite, not divide, us, she thought.

They traveled in a south-westerly direction along the Arkansas River on the Santa Fe Trail toward the Great Bend over a beautiful, level, and grassy plain. In the distance, rugged, snow-capped mountains could be seen jutting up into a cerulean blue sky.

Early one morning when Olive was fetching water from the river, she came upon Robert Kelly. He was standing under a tall tree, sharpening a straight-edged razor on a strop fastened to a low limb. Nailed to the trunk of the tree was a small, rectangular metal mirror. As she watched from the cover of some thimbleberry bushes, Robert reached down and picked up a pottery cup. He poured some water from a kettle into the cup, then mixed the ingredients with a small brush and began to apply a thick, soapy lather to his face. His legs were splayed apart to give him firm purchase on the rough gravel of the riverbank. His suspenders hung down along the sides of his trousers. Above the waistband, his naked torso rose, revealing the strong muscles of his broad-shouldered back.

She drew in her breath sharply, and for a while, she was mesmerized as he skillfully dragged the sharp razor over his face and neck, removing layers of soapy lather along with the remnants of his ruddy beard. She had never seen a man shave before. Her father had a full, black beard which he occasionally trimmed, but never shaved.

Then, as if sensing her presence, or perhaps catching a glimpse of her in the mirror, he turned his head, looked over his shoulder, and broke into a grin. Lather still clung to half of his face

"Like what you see?" he asked.

Olive's face burned in embarrassment. She turned and ran toward camp, spilling water from her bucket along the way, while the sound of Robert's hearty laughter rang in her ears.

The children walked alongside the wagons most of the time, climbing into the wagons only when their energy flagged. A few days after Olive was caught staring at Robert while he shaved; she was walking briskly over the short, green grass, singing hymns to keep from getting tired, when Robert rode up beside her, swept her up into his saddle, and proceeded to race ahead at a gallop. Robert took the reins in his right hand and lowered his left arm diagonally in front of Olive, pulling her close to him. He then lowered his head and, taking advantage of the stiff breeze that blew her long, dark hair back, kissed her ear. She turned and gave him a reproving look.

"Robert, stop that! They'll see us," she shouted.

"So what?" he replied, laughing.

He increased his grip on her, forcing her body against his, and, despite her protests, she found herself enjoying a sensation she had never experienced before. She wondered what James Brewster would say if he saw them. Certainly anything this delicious had to be sinful.

When they turned and rode back to join the others, Olive was conscious of several furtive glances cast in their direction, but most of them were smiling. She smiled back.

One morning, while at camp on the river, Olive and Mary Ann became bored.

"Olie, there's nothing to do. Can we play a game?"

"Mother says we aren't allowed to go too far from camp", said Olive.

Just then, Mr. Mutere walked by on his way to the river to draw some water. He was whistling a lively tune, and the girls paused in their conversation to watch him pass. He was a rather comic figure, short and bow-legged, with a prominent Adam's apple and a head shaped like a pumpkin. His eyes protruded from their sockets like two boiled onions, and his thin, bony arms hung from his soiled vest like two pipe cleaners. He was the perfect target for a practical joke. The girls followed him and hid behind a little mound near the river. He filled his bucket, and as he headed back to camp, Olive and Mary Ann pulled their aprons over their heads, jumped up from behind their hiding place, and began whooping wildly. Mr. Mutere went running into camp, yelling, "Injuns, Injuns!"

He went headlong over a wagon tongue, his tin pail clanging as it rolled, setting the watchdogs barking and howling, alerting the entire camp. Olive and Mary Ann came into camp, laughing and falling all over each other. They were sternly reprimanded by their parents and sent to sit in the wagon until they were called for supper. Mr. Mutere was the butt of jokes throughout the camp for the remainder of the day.

One Saturday evening, the tents were pitched on the banks of the Arkansas River. The next morning, being the Sabbath, the Reverend Brewster conducted services. At the termination of worship hour, Mr. Mutere crossed the river a short distance from the camp to look after the stock. Suddenly, wild, crude music intruded on the Sunday morning silence. Proceeding stealthily to a nearby grove of trees, he perceived a band of Indians engaged in a victory celebration of some kind. They were chanting and dancing. He recognized them to be Comanche. He saw among them a number of beautiful American horses and mules. He knew they were stolen, as they bore saddle and harness marks. While he stood motionless, his heart began to pound as he saw, emerging from behind a tree, a huge, painted buck. In his hands, he held a rifle leveled at Mutere's chest.

Terrified, Mutere took off on a run toward camp. The Indian stepped out of the shadow of the trees and began hallooing to Mutere, professing friendship. Mutere continued to run. As soon as he reached camp, several Indians appeared on the opposite bank of the river, hallooing, professing friendship, and requesting to be allowed to come into camp. After some consideration, their request was granted, and about ten of them came up near the camp. The settlers were apprehensive. This was their first encounter with Indians.

Almost immediately, the Brewsterites realized their mistake in allowing the Indians into camp, as they stood apart and appeared to be holding a secret council, furtively eyeing the women and children and sizing up the livestock, all the while flexing their bows and arrows. The settlers went instantly to their guns, taking up positions on the opposite side of the wagons. The women and children took cover except for a few of the women who were handy with a rifle. They joined the men in preparation for a fight.

Seeing their determination to defend themselves and their possessions, the Indians lowered their bows and their few guns and modestly made a request for a cow. The demand was quickly and emphatically denied.

Now the Indians showed signs of fear and they soon departed. A few hours later, they again appeared on the opposite riverbank with a score of fine animals, which they drove to water within sight of the settlers. As soon as the stock had been watered, the Indians raised a loud whoop, gave a few blood-curdling yells, and were away to the south at breakneck speed.

As the last sound of the Indians' cries and hoofbeats faded away in the distance, Robert Kelly was the first to speak.

"We'd better be off at first light. They'll be back with reinforcements. We're a juicy plum waiting to be plucked."

The Brewsterites hastily broke camp and were off at first light in the morning. They crossed the river and, toward evening, met a government train that had been out to Fort Yuma and was now on its return to Independence, Missouri. They came into camp and joined the Brewsterites for supper. Around the campfire, their captain reported that a day or two before, they had come upon the remnants of a government train which had been on its way to the fort. He said, "Their stock had been stolen and the members had been massacred. One man survived long enough to tell us that the Indians had taken a woman prisoner. Her name is Mrs. Snow."

The Brewsterites sat in shocked silence. Finally, Mrs. Wilder spoke.

"Oh, dear Lord, that poor Mrs. Snow must have spent the night right across the river from us, within light of our own campfire."

Olive felt a chill. She turned to Lucy.

"There but for the grace of God go I," she whispered.

Members of the government train warned the Brewsterites that, the next day, they would enter a desert and for ninety miles would be without wood or water. The Brewsterites immediately set about making preparations to cross this "Sahara" of the old Santa Fe Road. They filled buckets of water from the river and gathered all the firewood they could carry.

However, as far as water was concerned, these precautions proved unnecessary, as the clouds opened up, the rain poured down on them, and an abundance of fresh water became available. They considered this an unexpected blessing, though the livestock suffered for lack of forage.

Scattered along the trail, the bleached bones of dead livestock gave silent testimony to the perils of undertaking this inhospitable stretch of land in warm weather without sufficient water.

After crossing the big desert, a humorous incident occurred. Two men were out hunting when they came upon a large herd of antelope, which they began to chase in the direction of the camp. Several boys and girls were out playing when they saw the herd coming and decided to help the hunters. They ran toward the herd, shouting and waving their arms to frighten the antelope back toward the hunters. However, the hunters, seeing the children come over the rise, mistook them for Indians. They abandoned the hunt and ran toward camp by a circuitous route, where they discovered they had been running from their own children.

Chapter VI
Dissention in the Ranks

The trip along the Cimarron Cutoff from the Great Bend of the Arkansas River to Moro, the first settlement they reached in New Mexico, was about five hundred miles. During this time, nothing of special interest occurred to break the monotony, except for the "grape dumpling affair."

Near a small creek, the settlers came upon a wild grape vineyard. Mrs. Mutere decided to bake grape dumplings, which she stored in a compartment at the rear of her wagon, intending to treat the hungry travelers at a future date. However, during the night, one of the men, Mr. A. P., with a reputation as a glutton, stole to the rear of Mrs. Mutere's wagon and emptied the grape dumplings into a sack, which he took to his wagon and consumed in one night. The next morning, Mrs. Mutere discovered her dumplings missing. Coincidentally, the glutton was very sick. Mrs. Mutere seized a stake and caned Mr. A. P. through the entire camp.

At Moro, a small town of about three hundred inhabitants comprised of a dilapidated Catholic mission and a fort garrisoned by Mexican soldiers, they were pleasantly surprised to see a fine stream that came, cool and clear, down the mountainside.

Here the grateful travelers stocked their wagons with fruits, vegetables, corn, and mutton.

When the Brewsterites arrived in the Mexican settlements, their store of meat was almost exhausted. However, at every village, an abundance of fresh mutton was available. It was of superior quality, and prices were low. Therefore, mutton was the mainstay of their diet for several hundred miles in this region.

In order to converse with the Mexicans, it became necessary to learn rudimentary Spanish, and, as a matter of survival, many of the emigrants became fairly fluent in the language. Some had brought

English/Spanish phrase books with them in anticipation of the language barrier, although the inquiry *"Habla inglés?"* usually produced someone who could speak a little English, particularly in those villages where American wagon trains habitually stopped. The Yankee dollar was strong motivation for the Mexicans to learn basic English. When buyers and sellers came together, they somehow managed to consummate the transaction, regardless of language disparities.

Again, disagreements and disaffection began to surface among the Brewsterites. Harsh reality had set in, and the conduct of their leaders became suspect and self-serving. Whatever charisma James Brewster had appeared to possess now faded under the close scrutiny of his disillusioned followers.

Olive was warned to steer clear of James Brewster, as a rumor had been circulating around the camp that he had made advances toward one of the young girls. However, it was impossible to avoid him altogether. One evening, after everyone had retired to their wagons, Olive remembered to feed the dogs. As she gathered the leftover scraps from dinner, he came up behind her, startling her and causing her to drop the bowl of scraps, spilling them on the ground.

"How are you this fine evening, my child?" Something about his voice made her recoil. His face smiled, while eyes did not. He came closer until there was barely any space between them. Olive was uncomfortable, but before she could back away, he reached out and grasped her arm.

Then, from the shadows, a deep voice commanded, "Let her go, Brewster."

Robert Kelly stepped forward into the glow of the dying campfire.

James Brewster dropped his hand to his side.

"Just watching out for Miss Olive. Not safe being out here alone at night. Might be Injuns about."

"There are some things worse than Injuns, Reverend—like men who profess to be god-fearin' protectors of women but prey on them instead."

"How dare you make assertions about my character? I am a man of God."

"Then act like one. If I see you touch Olive again, I'll whip you, man of God or no. And that goes for any other female in this train. Keep your hands off them, Brewster."

Olive stood frozen to the spot as James Brewster slowly backed away, turned, and walked briskly toward his wagon.

"Evenin', Olive," said Robert lifting his hat and grinning broadly.

Still shaken, Olive looked up at Robert.

"Thank you," she whispered, barely able to speak. Then, remembering the scraps scattered on the ground, she stooped to pick them up, but Robert got there first. He quickly gathered them and handed her the bowl.

"They're a tad grubby, but the dogs won't mind. I'll be turnin' in now," he said. He tipped his hat and walked off into the darkness.

Olive stood staring after him for a moment before she remembered the waiting dogs and walked around the back of the wagon to feed them.

The following morning, they came to the Natural, or Santa Fe, Pass and camped at a place called The Forks. From this point, there is one trail leading in a southerly direction, known as the Cook-Kearny Route, and another leading in a northwesterly direction toward Santa Fe, which would later be named the Butterworth Trail. This emigrant route would not be known as the Butterworth Trail until September 15, 1857, when John Warren Butterfield, in partnership with Wells Fargo, established it as a mail route between St. Louis and San Francisco.

By this time, the disagreements had accelerated to the point that it was impossible for the group to remain together. Ultimately, the final break came over trail leadership, rather than religious penchants. As the men sat around the campfire that evening after the women and children had retired, the discussion became heated. One man spoke up.

"Folks in Las Vegas say the trail between here and Santa Fe is covered with sand. It could be hard going with the animals and the wagons, and if we can't see the trail, we could get lost."

Brewster snapped back, "Well, it's the way we're going—isn't that right, Mr. Goodale?"

"Yes, sir, Reverend, best to stick to the Santa Fe Trail. It's the way most folks go," said Goodale.

There was grumbling, and some nods of agreement. Royce Oatman spoke up.

"I'll be taking the southern route by way of the San Pedro and Santa Cruz Rivers. We'll go through Socorro and then take the Cooke-Kearney Cutoff to the Gila Trail. Those that wish to follow me should make their desires known first thing in the morning."

So it was that on the morning of October 9, 1850, thirty people in twelve wagons, led by James Brewster, took the northwesterly route to Santa Fe, while the remainder, consisting of eight wagons and twenty-two people, led by Royce Oatman, headed south on the Cooke-Kearney trail. It was a rough trail that had been blazed by Lieutenant Colonel Phillip St. George Cooke, a government surveyor, and General Stephen W. Kearney during the Mexican-American war. No emigrant party had ever traveled this trail before.

James Brewster would later announce that he had abandoned his intention of founding his colony, which he called "Bashan," at the mouth of the Colorado River. Instead, he would end his journey at Santa Fe. He would finally locate his religious community, Colonia, seven miles south of Socorro Peak.

Coincidentally, the Oatman party had decided to go on to California, several of them having been infected with gold fever. Oatman began to refer to their new destination as "Lahoga," his name for the Promised Land.

Following Oatman's wagon were seven others. The occupants were as follows: Mr. and Mrs. Ira Thompson and daughters, Susan and Lucy; Mr. and Mrs. Willard Wilder and their eighteen-month old son, J. C.; the Kelly brothers, John Z. and Robert; Mr. and Mrs. Brimhall; Mr. and Mrs. Mutere; Dr. and Mrs. Lane; Dr. Lane's brother and niece, Isabel; and Mr. and Mrs. Cheesbrough.

Oatman's group headed south on the Cooke-Kearney route and, for a while, grass for the teams was more plentiful than for the previous hundred miles. When they neared the village of La Joya, the *alcalde* (mayor) came out to greet them with an armed guard to escort them into town. Ira Thompson wrote in a letter, "The people here are remarkably kind to us."

On October 19th, the Oatman wagon train crossed the Rio Grande. Here, they rested their teams for three days, though they were concerned that any delays would further deplete their meager supplies

When they reached Socorro, a Mexican military post, they reveled in the feeling of security it provided. For a while, they could enjoy freedom from the fear of Indian attacks. It was a beautiful but poor Mexican settlement. The countryside was barren of food, but abundant in hostile Indians. They spent a week at Socorro, during which they and the animals rested while they attempted to replenish their fast-diminishing supplies.

They soon learned that food was becoming scarce among the settlements that lay along their path. Price and quantity were serious issues, and their money was running out.

It was from Socorro on October 26, 1850, that Ira Thompson wrote a letter to *The Olive Branch,* a four-page family newspaper published in Boston.

> Jackson Goodale was chosen leader, which proved disadvantageous to the company. On the ninth day of October, Royce Oatman was chosen leader to fill the place which J. Goodale was first chosen to fill.
> The party divided about a hundred miles from Santa Fe on the ninth day of October. Thirty-two went with Brewster for Santa Fe, and the rest started for California with Royce Oatman.

They left Socorro on November 10th and traveled south along the Rio Grande through the dry desert area called *Journada del Muerto* (Journey of the Dead). Here, they encountered many discouraging difficulties. Sections of the country were barren. Their teams were failing. As if this weren't enough, encounters with hostile Indians were becoming more and more frequent and alarming. The children were cautioned against straying far from the wagons

About ninety-five miles south of Socorro, they left the Rio Grande. They headed southwest on Cooke's Wagon Road, where they began their ascent through the mountains toward Guadalupe Pass.

A few days after leaving the Rio Grande, Mr. A. W. Lane died of the mountain fever. His nineteen-year-old daughter Mary had died of tuberculosis at the outset of the journey, leaving one surviving daughter, Isabel, to travel on with her aunt and uncle, Dr. and Mrs. Lane. Mr. Lane had been well liked among the members of the wagon train, and they mourned his loss. They dug a grave on one of the foothills, and after a short funeral; his body was lowered into it. Some of the women planted flowers on the grave, and a crude stake inscribed with his name and date of death was hammered into the earth.

Then they passed through a mountainous region where the severe ascents and steep declivities were more taxing on the teams than any previous travel. They were required to fell trees and tie them to the rear of the wagons to act as brakes. A great deal of time was lost making culverts and searching for safe fording places. They often advanced a mere four or five miles a day.

On November 22, the emigrants were reminded that it was dangerously late in the year to be crossing a mountain range in northern Mexico when they awoke to see snow on the surrounding hills. Olive wrapped herself in her blankets, but she was still dreadfully cold. Then she noticed a few snowflakes, then several more, and soon, there was an inch of snow on the ground. Everyone huddled in the wagons, and soon it stopped snowing, but they were all cold, hungry, and thirsty. They had spent the previous day and night without firewood or water.

As they gathered up their stock, which had scattered during the night in search of forage, one of the men noticed a streak of timber coming down the side of a distant mountain. He shouted, "Look! Trees!"

They immediately set off in that direction, and after almost a full day, during which they suffered severely from cold and thirst, their efforts were rewarded. Not only did they find timber and a stream of fresh water, but a plentiful supply of fish and game. Wild turkey, antelope, deer, and sheep bounded through the lush woodland.

They quickly built a blazing fire and heated the icy water so it was drinkable and comforting. They gave thanks to God for leading them to this magical place. If they had not found it, they would surely have perished. They remained here for a week until they were well rested and the teams were growing fat on the rich pasturage.

On the third day of their stay, a group of ragged Indian women and children emerged from the forest, suddenly materializing out of the early morning mist. They kept a respectable distance from the camp, silently observing the emigrants. Mrs. Wilder was the first to notice them. She turned to Mary Ann Oatman.

"Look, the poor things are starving. The smell of food must have drawn them. It would be cruel to turn them away."

As the two women observed their silent visitors, Mrs. Thompson joined them. "We could cook a few extra pots of beans and put them out where they can eat without fear of being driven off," she said.

"It's the Christian thing to do," said Mrs. Oatman.

That being settled, they quickly set about putting pots of beans where they could be seen by the visitors. The Indians advanced tentatively, but upon reaching the fragrant, steaming pots, all inhibitions vanished as they satisfied their hunger. When they had finished, they vanished into the woods as suddenly as they had appeared. They came again the next day, and the Brewsterite women were ready for them, having cooked many extra pots of beans. The following morning, a few braves and two old men came with the women and children. The next day, no one came. The Brewsterites waited with many extra pots of beans, but there was no one to eat them.

Early the following morning, Olive was fetching water from the stream when she saw three fierce-looking Indians approaching. Their faces were painted, and they carried bows and arrows. Instinct told her they were not merely hunters. She ran through the camp, alerting everyone. The Indians entered the camp, smiling and professing friendship while they surreptitiously appraised the horses, oxen, and cattle. The Brewsterites quickly took up their guns and, brandishing them at the Indians, drove them off.

Taking no chances, the men took turns standing guard that night. No one slept. Everyone kept their muskets primed and close at hand. The dogs kept up a continuous clamor, barking and growling all through the night.

The next morning, it was clear what the Indians had been up to. Their tracks were everywhere, and, although they were gone, they had taken twenty head of cattle, four oxen, and one mare with them. Olive watched as the men left camp in search of the stolen livestock, but returned empty-handed. They had followed the tracks to a deep canyon where it would have been foolish to proceed.

The snow had melted, and the emigrants decided to break camp and leave before the Indians returned. Now they were forced to leave some wagons, food, and belongings behind due to the shortage of animals. The Oatmans still had their wagon, but only one team of oxen, two cows, and two horses. This meant that the animals could not be spared to rest, no matter how worn out they became. Furthermore, the protection afforded by a defensive circle of many wagons was no longer an option. The little party was now extremely vulnerable to an Indian attack.

Chapter VII
The Fatal Decision

Once they were clear of the mountains, they passed through a rich pasturage country with the most delightful scenery since they had left the Big Bend. They arrived at Santa Cruz, Sonora, Mexico, on Christmas Day, 1850, in better spirits and with more vigorous teams than they had experienced in the past few hundred miles.

Santa Cruz was a lovely little village of about a hundred inhabitants. The tired, hungry Americans were welcomed by the Mexican residents as reinforcements. They told the emigrants that the Apaches feared the American guns and excellent marksmanship. The Mexicans begged them to stay. However, there was nothing to eat but pumpkins, as the Indians had taken everything else. The Americans moved on, not only because of the food shortage, but due to the urgings of Royce Oatman, whose gold fever had replaced his religious fervor. He had stopped referring to "Lahoga" as the Promised Land.

Now they were forced to live off the land and whatever they could dig or kill on this barren stretch. Royce Oatman rationed the remaining biscuits at the rate of one and a half per person per day. They supplemented this with hawk and coyote soup. Susan Thompson later recalled that her mother had become quite ill after trying to eat coyote soup.

Olive desperately searched the wagon for something to eat. Her efforts were rewarded when she lifted a floorboard and found two small burlap sacks. One contained a few cups of barley, and the other held about a pound of dried apple slices. She quickly mixed the two ingredients with a small amount of water and cooked the mixture over the glowing coals of the evening campfire. This mixture fed their family of nine for two days. They thanked Olive for this unexpected bounty, and all agreed that it was the tastiest dish they had ever eaten. Lorenzo remarked, "It isn't as good as pot roast, but it's much better than coyote soup."

When they reached Tubac, they were on the brink of starvation. Mrs. Oatman was in the advanced stages of pregnancy, and there was great anxiety regarding her health and the health of her unborn child.

The first day after their arrival in Tubac, Mrs. Mutere, a rather obese woman, was walking about the compound headed toward the community well. In order to avoid the well, she stepped to the side of it, and the ground below her suddenly caved in, trapping her huge, flailing body in waist-high muddy water. To the astonishment of the locals, great amounts of water began to gush forth. It seemed she had fallen into an abandoned well that had not been used since the new one was dug.

Supplies were sparse in Tubac, and the little wagon train moved on to Tukjon (Tucson), where they hoped to find enough food and water to take them on to Fort Yuma.

They arrived in Tukjon on January 8, 1851. Susan Thompson, in her diary, clearly recalls this date, as it was her eighteenth birthday. Tukjon was more pleasantly and securely situated, with an elevation of about three thousand feet. More importantly, the emigrants were able to secure food. Shortly after their arrival, Mr. Brimhall mistakenly mentioned that he was a "Yankee," meaning that he was an American. However, the Mexican-American war[1] had ended just three years earlier, and the atrocities committed by a renegade company of soldiers calling themselves "the Yankee Volunteers" were fresh in the minds of the Mexicans. They refused to supply the Brimhalls with food or lodging. The other emigrants had to smuggle food to them from their own allotments.

When an old Mexican man's foot became infected from an imbedded mesquite thorn, Susan Thompson made a poultice of sugar and white of egg which drew the thorn out. When the old man recovered, the general attitude toward the visitors changed for the better. The old Mexican rented a house to the Thompsons, and his wife insisted on doing their washing.

The Mexicans had been amazed by the "magic" of Susan's poultice. However, when Susan was able to go outside the town and call her cattle to her, they were convinced she had supernatural powers. They had never heard of controlling their animals by kindness.

Now their hosts implored the "Americanos" to stay to strengthen the isolated pueblo. This time, the emigrants listened. It was, indeed, an excellent place to raise grain and graze cattle. The entire wagon train halted here for a month. Five families decided to stay for a year and had made arrangements for farming here. They were the Thompsons, the Muteres, the Brimhalls, the Lanes, and the Cheesbroughs.

After a month's rest, Royce Oatman was determined to press on. Only the Wilders and the Kellys were willing to follow. They moved on, despite many difficulties, for several days. Their provisions had been poorly replenished in Tukjon, although the inhabitants had done all in their power to provide them with food. However, they too had suffered crop losses as a result of Apache raids.

The small party staggered across the ninety-mile desert via Picacho Peak and Casa Grande. This was the most barren and desolate region they had traveled thus far. Their oxen were emaciated and supplies exhausted. Frequently, they were wakened to arm themselves against the approaching Apaches who tracked them at the front and rear of their small wagon train for days.

Weary and heartsick, they arrived at the relative safety of the Pima and Maricopa Indian villages. This little settlement of Pima Indians was engaged in constant hostilities with the Apaches. So far, they had been able to hold them off by their skill and determination to survive. However, they had been fighting off the Apaches so long that they were short of provisions and nearly destitute.

The Pimas had been farming here for many years, but during the past two years, the constant enemy raids had seriously curtailed their activities, resulting in sparse crops and a food shortage. The Pimas warned them of Apaches along the Gila Trail ahead.

After a brief consultation, the Wilders and the Kellys decided to remain in Pimole until such time as they might receive supplies from government or friends. They planned to wait and join the next wagon train to come through this route.

Royce Oatman considered going on alone. The Wilders and the Kellys implored him to remain in the Pima village with them, citing the danger of traveling alone through Apache country.

A few days later, when it appeared futile to dissuade Royce Oatman from going on alone, Mrs. Wilder, half running, strode briskly across the dusty camp.

"Captain Oatman!" she shouted.

Royce turned and waited for her to approach him.

"Mrs. Wilder," he said by way of acknowledgement.

She was a tall woman and stood eye to eye with Oatman. She was clearly agitated. Her hands, held tightly at her sides, were balled up in fists. Her face, usually cheerful, was creased by a disapproving frown.

"Captain Oatman, I've come to beg you not to leave. Your wife is very close to her time. If you leave now, she might have to give birth on the desert in harsh conditions. I've been told there's a midwife here in the village. She is said to be very good. Mary Ann would be made comfortable, and I would be happy to assist in any way I can."

For a long moment, Royce stared at her. Finally, he spoke.

"Do you think I want my child to come into the world among savages? Surely you don't think I would entrust my wife to a heathen, nor would I want my child touched by one. We'll take our chances, and, with God's help, she'll have the child at Fort Yuma, attended by the fort physician."

Mrs. Wilder stood looking at him in disbelief, her face red with anger

"You're a fool … no, worse than a fool. You're a stubborn, selfish brute. May God have mercy on your poor family. I'll pray that you change your mind."

With a parting sigh of exasperation, she turned and, clutching her long skirt, walked quickly back to her wagon, muttering to herself.

For a while, Royce considered his options. The thought of 190 miles of desert and mountains with scarce forage for the animals, now reduced to two yoke of cows and one yoke of oxen, was daunting. On the other hand, if they remained, they might starve or perhaps be killed by Apaches.

While he remained in this perplexed condition, Dr. John Lawrence Le Conte, an entomologist, and his Mexican guide, Manuel, came into the Pima village. Le Conte said he had passed the entire distance to Fort Yuma and back without encountering a single Indian. Nor did he see any indication of the proximity of Indians along the Gila Trail. Based on this information, Royce Oatman made his final decision.

That night, while Olive was preparing to turn in, Robert Kelly appeared at the side of the Oatmans' wagon.

"Olive, please listen to me. I have a bad feeling about this. You must convince your father to stay. It's too dangerous to travel across the desert alone."

"Robert, I trust my father's judgment. All I can do is pray that he's made the right decision. I'm sorry you won't be with us, but perhaps we'll meet again someday in California."

"Good-bye, Olive. I wish you well. No matter what happens, I'll never forget you." He kissed her cheek and walked quickly toward his wagon.

Later, as she lay down on her bedroll, Olive thought about Robert's warning and his good-bye kiss. She was disturbed by the finality of it. She thought about speaking to her father, but she knew it was useless. Once he made up his mind, there was no changing it. She prayed, but was not comforted.

On the 8th of February, 1851, the little family rode out of the Pima village with their small team and one wagon. Royce Oatman was disappointed in the Wilders and the Kellys. No one had come out to say good-bye and wish them well. This stung him deeply. He had been their captain and therefore deserving of their respect and loyalty. However, he still had his family, and they trusted and believed in him. This comforted him and tempered his bitter disappointment in his friends.

They were exhausted by the long journey they had completed thus far, and they were frightened by the danger this long, lonely expanse presented. Nevertheless, Royce Oatman had made his decision, and nothing could change his mind.

For six days, they traveled southwest at a tortuous pace over a barren landscape. Occasionally, a Saguaro cactus rose high above them, but otherwise, a scattering of mesquite was the only relief from the bleak, rocky terrain. The going was difficult, and the oxen were failing.

On the seventh day, while attempting to goad their worn-out oxen over a particularly hazardous area, they were overtaken by Dr. Le Conte and his Mexican guide, Manuel, who were heading back to Fort Yuma, a distance of about 140 miles from their present location. They were riding horses and could travel the distance in a much shorter time than the Oatmans.

Dr. Le Conte immediately saw the pitiful condition of the family.

"Mr. Oatman, I suggest you write a letter to Major Heintzelman at Fort Yuma and ask for assistance. I will deliver it immediately upon my arrival at the fort. I have paper, pen, and ink in my pack."

Oatman then sat down and composed a letter which read as follows:

> February 15th, 1851 at camp on the Hila (Gila) River
> To the honorable commandant of Fort Yuma, Brevett
> Major S. P. Heintzelman
>
> Honorable Sir: I am under the necessity of calling upon you for assistance. There is myself, wife, and seven children, and without help, sir, I am confident we must perish.
> I cannot accurately give our position. I have naught but scarce provisions, sir. I wish you to send four horses with harness for two. I have gear for one. I will meet your men as near to your camp as possible. I am now, sir, about 140 miles from your camp. I have been robbed of my animals, so that I have not sufficient in their present

condition to take me through. I send this by Dr. John
Le Conte in haste.

Yours with due respect.
Royce Oatman

Dr. Le Conte took the letter, placed it in his pack, and assured
Oatman, "I will proceed as quickly as I can to the fort, and I will do all
in my power to procure help at once."

He and his guide, Manuel, soon left the Oatmans and headed for
Fort Yuma.

The little family watched them ride out of sight and prayed they
would have a safe and expeditious journey.

About sunset of the day after they left the Oatmans, Dr. Le Conte
and Manuel had gone about thirty miles when they turned their horses
into a small valley hemmed in by high mountains. They slept until
daybreak and began making preparations for the day's ride to Fort
Yuma.

Suddenly, twelve Yuma Indians emerged from behind a bluff and
boldly entered the camp. Dr. Le Conte went for his pistol. While he and
Manuel kept a close eye on them, the Indians began to walk about
nonchalantly while one of them drew the doctor into conversation in the
Spanish language. Their evil intentions soon became apparent as they
proceeded to surround the doctor and his guide. Manuel brandished a
knife and leapt to one side, shouting, "Shoot! Shoot!"

But the doctor held his fire. The Indians then put on a pretense of
friendliness as they attempted to persuade Dr. Le Conte of their good
intentions. Manuel, angered by the Indians' treachery, leapt into the air
and was about to plunge his knife into the leader of the band, but was
stopped by Dr. Le Conte.

"No, Manuel," he commanded with a coolness he didn't really feel.
The Indians were impressed with his show of courage despite the
odds.

Manuel, enraged by their insolence, continued to spring into the air, screaming at the top of his lungs, *"Pero! Pero!"* The Indians soon departed.

When Doctor Le Conte and Manuel went into the valley to retrieve their animals, they discovered that the twelve Yumas had enacted the scene in the camp as a distraction while another group of the same band stole their horses and mules. They were forced to proceed to Fort Yuma on foot. However, before he left, Dr. Le Conte posted a card on a tree near the trail, warning the Oatmans of the proximity of the Indians and relating what had befallen him and Manuel. He reassured the Oatmans that he would proceed immediately to the fort to secure help for them. Dr. Le Conte then hid his saddle and packages in a secluded place and resumed his journey.

Unfortunately, the Oatmans missed seeing the card, although they camped at the very spot where the Doctor and Manuel had encountered the Indians. It was later found by the Kellys and the Wilders. Had the Oatmans seen the card, they might have turned back.

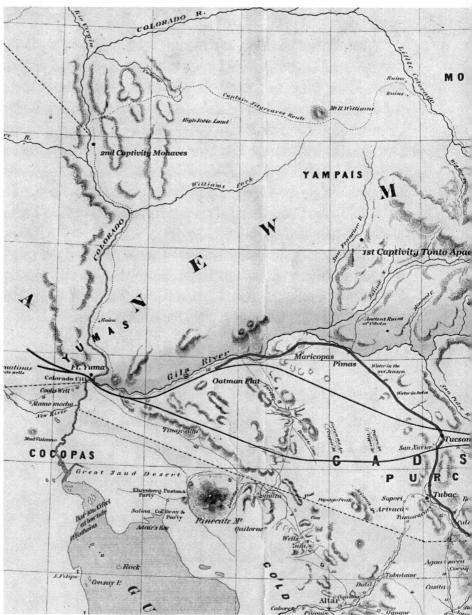

Adapted from Ehrenberg Map, 1854

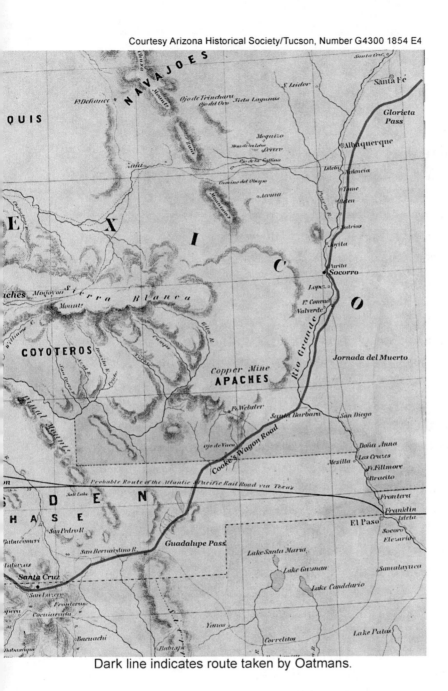

Dark line indicates route taken by Oatmans.

Chapter VIII
The Massacre

On the evening of February 17th, 1851, the Oatman family reached the Gila River at a point over eighty miles from Pimole and about the same distance from Fort Yuma. They descended to the river from a high bluff and looked for a safe place to cross. At one point, the river divided, leaving a small sandbar in the middle of the stream. The area was wild and rough, and it was impossible to see for a distance in any direction. The river was swollen by early spring run-off and was extraordinarily wide and deep.

They attempted to cross the Gila at sunset. They struggled frantically with frightened oxen, pushing and pulling the wagon until everyone was in a state of exhaustion. Finally, they reached the sand island in the middle of the river, where the teams mired, the wagon dragged, and it was impossible to proceed.

They detached the teams and prepared to spend the night on the island. As darkness fell and the wind began to howl, Royce Oatman waded across a shallow area of the river to find firewood. It was late on that cold, windy night before a camp-fire was struck. In the flickering light from the fire, the dejected countenance of their father had a chilling effect on the children. They had never seen him like this. Mother tried to maintain a cheerful demeanor as she prepared a meager meal of biscuits and bean soup.

Later that night, the children huddled in their blankets, unable to sleep. They exchanged thoughts about their situation and began to discuss what they would do in the event of an Indian attack.

"I would get Papa's gun and shoot them," said Lorenzo.

"I would run and hide," said Mary Ann.

"I would kill myself," said Olive.

Then Lucy spoke in a soft, terrified voice.

"I heard Papa crying last night. He told Mama that he felt something terrible was about to happen. He said he felt it. Mama tried to comfort him, but he kept crying. He kept saying, 'What have I done? What have I done?'"

The children looked at each other, their eyes wide with fear. The wind howled louder, and the river lapped at the remnants of their little campfire. They did not sleep well that night.

The next morning, February 18, 1851, they arose feeling exhausted. Their limbs felt heavy, and they moved very slowly. Their father did not look at them. He busied himself with preparations to leave.

The teams were brought up from a small neck of land where they had found sparse pasturage during the night. They hitched the oxen to the wagon and soon made the opposite riverbank. Before them was a steep incline of some two hundred feet. They had advanced a short distance when the oxen refused to move. They were forced to unload everything from the wagon and carry it all to the top of the hill. The team still refused to drag the empty wagon to the summit.

When they finally prodded and cajoled the oxen to move, they reached the top of the mesa. Here they camped and remained during the heat of the day, intending to travel by moonlight that night.

About two hours before sunset, they started, and, just before the sun sank behind the western hills, they had made the ascent of another hill and gone about a mile. They halted here to reload the remainder of their baggage.

The children now noticed a great change in their father's demeanor. Whereas, he had always been cheerful and positive when faced with adversity, he now became withdrawn and morose. Mother appeared calm, administering to the comfort of her husband and children. If she was fearful or apprehensive, she gave no indication. The older children watched her closely for any sign of labor pains. She was, in fact, in the early stages of labor, but would not reveal this to the family for fear of inciting panic.

Suddenly, Royce sat down on a rock near the wagon and cried, "Mother, Mother, in the name of God, I know that something dreadful is about to happen."

Mother went to him and placed her hand on his shoulder.

"Royce, dear, everything will be all right. God will protect us and keep us safe. We will pray," she said. Then, gathering the children about her she said, "Children, let us ask the Lord to protect us from harm."

The little family bowed their heads and prayed, but the powerful grip of fear held them, even as they uttered the words of worship.

They soon reached the summit of a long, level mesa stretching westward. It lay between two deep gorges, one on the right and the other on the left. The Gila River ran through the gorge to their right. They hastily ate a meal of dry bread and bean soup in preparation for the night's travel. The nights were cool, a mercy to their weak, famished teams, and a full moon was expected which would provide light almost all night long. Time was of the essence now, as their provisions were seriously depleted

With the meal completed and the sun beginning to set behind a distant mountain peak, they were making preparations to resume travel over the wild, barren region. Royce, as in a trance, was loading some of the baggage on the wagon when Lorenzo turned and looked down the hill they had just ascended. For a moment, he was stunned. Then, pointing down the hill, he shouted, "Father! Look! Indians!"

Then he looked at his father's face, and what he saw frightened him more than the sight of the Indians.

There were seventeen of them. Most were naked, except for loincloths. Some wore wolf or coyote skins about their shoulders. All were filthy and disheveled. Their eyes blazed wildly as they strode boldly into camp.

Royce Oatman, his face a grey mask, fought to gain control of his fear. The muscles in his face began to spasm uncontrollably. He spoke to his family in an effort to calm them.

"Don't be afraid. They won't hurt you."

Then, to the Indians he said in Spanish, "Sit down and have a smoke."

A few of the Indians understood him, and they sat down on rocks. Royce Oatman went to the wagon and brought out a pipe and some tobacco. He sat down with them, lit the pipe, and took a puff. Then he passed it to the Indian on his left, who smoked and passed the pipe down to the others. When all had smoked, they asked for food.

"I have only enough for my family," he said.

They became angry. Royce again went to the wagon and brought back some bread. When they had eaten that, they demanded more.

"If I give you more, my family will starve," he replied.

Now the Indians stood up and walked to one side in a huddle, consulting one another in loud, agitated tones. They spoke in the Apache language, which the Oatmans did not understand.

The family was terrified. They began to go through the motions of loading the wagon and preparing to leave. Mr. Oatman had again returned to complete the reloading of the wagon. Mrs. Oatman was in the wagon, arranging the items as he passed them to her. Olive was standing on the side of the wagon opposite the Indians with Lucy and the younger children. Mary Ann sat on a stone, holding a rope attached to the horns of the foremost team. Lorenzo was helping his father.

Suddenly, there was a horrible shriek, and the Indians leapt into the air shouting, *"Yakoa! Yakoa!"*

They produced war clubs from under their wolfskins and ran, screaming and swinging their clubs, toward Royce Oatman. Lorenzo was the first to fall to the ground under a blow from a war club. Later, they took his hat and shoes and dragged him to the brink of the hill by his feet. Olive was sure they would throw him over the edge to the rocks below, and she turned her head, unable to look.

Olive watched in horror as a huge, painted buck lunged at her elder sister, Lucy, ripping the front of her dress from neck to waist. She screamed and raked the left side of his face with her fingernails. He put his hand to his face, and when he drew it away and saw his blood-stained fingers, his face contorted in rage. He uttered a guttural sound like a wounded animal and bent quickly to pick up his club. As he straightened up, Lucy kicked him in the crotch with her steel-toed boot, sending him backward, clutching his crotch and howling. He regained his footing, lunged forward, and swung his club with tremendous force, crushing the side of Lucy's face. She fell to her knees, and her attacker raised his club and lowered it squarely in the center of her head, splitting her skull with a dull, cracking sound. Olive screamed and vomited into the hard-packed sand.

Royce, Jr., a happy, playful child of six years, stood horrorstruck as he witnessed the commencement of the carnage, being furthest from the Indians. Then, as they came to him, he gave one piercing scream and sank to the earth under the club. Olive saw him go into convulsions. Then, with a moan and a heaving of his chest, he sank into death.

Next to die was little C. A., almost four, who had been spared when he fell under the wagon's wheel at the outset of the journey. When her mother screamed, Olive turned and saw her, clasping her youngest child in her arms, with the blows of the war club falling upon her and the child. Olive tried to go to her, but was pushed roughly aside. She fainted. When she awoke, eight-year-old Mary Ann was standing next to her in shock. Her father was moaning in pain; her mother, still holding her youngest child, appeared dead, as did the child. Lucy, Royce, Jr. and C. A. were dead. Lorenzo lay still, face-down in the sand, bleeding from his head, his ears, and his nose.

The Indians looted the wagon, cutting up a mattress to watch the feathers fly. They ripped the cloth covering from the staves of the wagon, took off the wagon wheels, broke open boxes with rocks and clubs, and took whatever caught their fancy. These and whatever small amounts of food they could find were tied up in bundles to be packed on their backs. They cut the animals loose and dragged them off.

When they had finished their killing and plundering, they turned their attention to Olive and Mary Ann. Five of the Indians were put in charge of Olive and Mary Ann, while the others tended to the livestock and any other items they considered valuable. Olive screamed, "Kill me! Kill me!"

Then she remembered poor little Mary Ann standing beside her and stifled her cries with her hand.

The savages laughed wildly at Olive's grief. They took the girls' shoes and hats, then pushed them along before them. They descended the hill from which they had come and crossed the Gila River. They traveled about half a mile by a dim trail through a dark, rough, and narrow gorge until they came to an open place where there had been an Indian camp before. Here, the Indians took off their packs, struck a fire with flint and wild cotton, and prepared a meal.

They boiled some of the beans taken from the wagon and mixed flour with water to bake in the ashes. They offered some to Olive and Mary Ann in a taunting manner, jeering and making fun of every indication of grief shown by them. Olive and Mary Ann could not eat as they thought of their family lying exposed and bloody on the rocky mesa. Mary Ann clung to Olive, sobbing convulsively. She was immediately hushed by the brandishing of a war club over her head.

Chapter IX
Driven Like Dogs

After an hour's rest, they repacked and made preparations to proceed. It was apparent by the way the Indians kept glancing at the trail behind them that they were worried about being pursued. Perhaps they could not believe that the Oatmans would have been so foolish as to travel alone. Surely other wagons had been following behind them, or perhaps the Oatmans had fallen behind and the others would send someone back to help them when they failed to appear. At any rate, they were determined to get well away from the scene of their depredation. The two exhausted girls had to run to keep up the pace. Their feet bled from the jagged rocks. When they fell, or slowed down, they were whipped. If they cried out in pain because their feet hurt, they were beaten. They traveled through the night with no respite.

One of the Indians took the lead, followed by Olive and Mary Ann, bareheaded and shoeless. They kept a rapid pace, much beyond their strength, for several hours. If their pace slackened or they gave any indication of grief, their captors would threaten them with war clubs and scream *"Yakoa!"* in their ears. They traveled at the rate of four or five miles an hour. Their feet were lacerated and bleeding freely. Little Mary Ann soon became unable to proceed and sank to the ground.

"I can't go on, Olive," she said piteously.

After prodding and beating her, and finding this useless, they threatened to kill her, but she had become utterly fearless of death. Olive wished they would kill her too. Finally, one of the sturdier Indians dislodged his pack, handed it to another, and rudely threw Mary Ann over his shoulder. In this manner, they proceeded. Olive, her strength failing, felt she would soon succumb to exhaustion and faint. She was prepared to take the consequences. But concern for Mary Ann sustained her in the dark hours 'til midnight. Mary Ann was silent, and Olive managed to look into her face. Mary Ann seemed to be indifferent to everything about her, relieved of all care of life or death and content to remain that way.

They proceeded over small bluff points of high mountain chains and rough, winding valleys in a northeasterly direction. They halted for a few moments about the middle of the night but otherwise had no rest until noon of the next day, when they came upon a few acres of level, sandy soil with an occasional tree. High and seemingly impassible mountains hemmed them in on every side. Their captors seemed familiar with this place. Olive dragged herself up to the place of halt, praying that there would be no more travel that day.

They had rested about two hours when the rest of the band who had taken the stock joined them. They had with them two oxen and the horse. Olive later learned that the rest of the stock had been slaughtered and hung up to dry until a future expedition returned to retrieve them. Here, they immediately proceeded to butcher the two oxen, to the horror of Olive and Mary Ann, who had regarded them as family pets. They then sliced them up and packed the parcels in equal packages upon their backs. They broiled some of the meat on the fire and prepared a meal of this, with burnt dough and bean soup. They offered some to Olive and Mary Ann, who ate greedily. Never did a tender veal steak prepared at home taste better than the tough, stringy piece of meat. This, accompanied by burnt dough soaked in bean soup, constituted the meal. As tired as she was, Olive could not sleep due to the pain in her torn and bloody feet.

Again, the Indians endeavored to get Mary Ann to walk, but she could not, despite threats and beating, which she endured without a murmur. One of them again took her upon his shoulder, and they started. Olive had not gone far when she found it impossible to walk due to the soreness of her feet. They then tied pieces of leather on her feet. This relieved much of the pain, but she still suffered from thirst and overexertion. She was now able to keep up with the heavily burdened Indians. Then, for six hours, the Indians whipped Mary Ann into walking.

That night, they halted in a snug, dark ravine at about ten o'clock and made preparations for a night's stay. The girls were shown a soft place in the sand, given two of their own blankets, and directed to sleep there. Three Indians were designated to guard them. Soon, despite their physical suffering, they drifted off into a troubled sleep, during which scenes of the bloody massacre haunted their dreams.

Sometime during the night, Olive was awakened by the approach of one of the Indians

He clamped his hand over her mouth and was in the process of lowering his body onto hers when a huge buck seized him by his hair and pulled him to his feet. The big Indian proceeded to chastise Olive's would-be rapist, waking the entire camp. Olive later learned that she was more valuable to them as a virgin.

They were roused at daybreak and served a breakfast of beef, burnt dough, and beans. The sun was fully up when, like cattle, they were driven into another day's travel. That day, they traveled over the roughest terrain Olive would ever experience. She told Mary Ann that she would consent to being murdered, for she would not proceed. But this was not to be allowed by her captors. She was driven, pushed, and hauled along over rocks and gravel. It would be the most pain and suffering ever endured in her entire captivity.

About noon, they were surprised by a band of eleven Indians of another tribe. They emerged from behind a rocky point set out into a dark ravine through which the Apaches and their captives were passing. Every one of them was armed with bows and arrows. They were jabbering and gesturing in a most agitated manner, all the while staring at Olive. While some of them conversed with members of the Apache band, two of them stealthily crept around behind the Apaches, plainly showing by gestures and facial expressions their hostile intentions toward Olive and Mary Ann.

Though their captors watched closely, one of the visitors strung his bow and let fly an arrow at Olive. Fortunately, it pierced the skirt of her dress and left her unharmed. He was in the act of firing a second arrow when two Apaches sprang toward him with their clubs, while two snatched Olive and Mary Ann to one side, placing themselves between the girls and the drawn bow. By this time, a strong Apache had the hostile Indian in a firm grip, forcing him to desist. The remainder of the visiting band continued to exhibit hostile behavior, and it seemed likely that a general fight would ensue.

Olive would later learn that they were land pirates and that the Indian who had tried to kill her had lost a brother in a battle with whites on the Santa Fe Trail. He had sworn to avenge his brother's death by taking the blood of an American. This was later related to Olive, in Spanish, by one of her captors. Had the marauding band been larger, a serious battle would have ensued and Olive's life sacrificed to the avenging Indian. As words flew back and forth between the two bands, Olive felt little anxiety, as she was convinced that, sooner or later, she and Mary Ann would perish suddenly, or inch by inch.

They traveled until midnight, when their captors called a halt. There was little sleep for Olive and Mary Ann. They looked up at the stars.

"Look, Mary Ann. There's the Big Dipper, and there's the North Star. It makes me feel better knowing that our friends and dear aunt and uncle in Illinois might be looking up at the heavens and seeing the same stars."

"Oh, yes, Olive. I'm sure they are. Do you think they are thinking of us?"

"I know they are, Mary Ann. They love us and pray for us every night."

"If only they knew how much we need their prayers now."

Olive thought about Robert and wondered where he was. Did he know about the massacre? Had he heard about her capture? She hoped he would not come looking for her. These Apaches would kill him. They would also kill her and Mary Ann if they thought they had been discovered.

"I wonder if we'll ever see the folks from the wagon train again," she said.

"We will if we pray hard enough," said Mary Ann. She turned to look at Olive.

"Are you thinking about Robert? Do you love him, Olive?"

"I'm, not sure I know what love is yet, Mary Ann. I do miss him, though. He made me laugh. These savages are devoid of humor, unless they are mocking us." She looked over at Mary Ann. She was asleep. Olive snuggled against her and soon fell into an exhausted sleep punctuated by the moans and screams of her dying parents, brothers, and sisters.

Chapter X
The Tonto Apache Village

On the third day, they came upon a cluster of low *wickiups,* mound-shaped huts made of skins stretched over wooden frames, each having an entry near the ground. Their captors became animated and anxious. There were no creeks or rivers and no grass or timber—just sagebrush on a barren landscape. To Olive and Mary Ann, the sight of dwelling places, no matter how coarse and primitive, was a welcome sight after traveling two hundred miles in three days on foot.

They were ushered into their squalid camp amid shouts and song, wild dancing, and crude music. It soon became apparent that their captors had made themselves a name by their exploits of the past week. They had set upon a defenseless family of nine, wantonly slaughtered seven of them, and taken two little girls captive. They had plundered their wagon and now produced a few sacks of smoked, soot-covered cow meat, a few beans, a little clothing, and one horse. The main attraction was, of course, the two captives.

That night was consumed by chanting and wild, indecent dancing in celebration of the triumph achieved and the spoils taken. They placed Olive and Mary Ann in the center of a circle and danced around them wildly, shrieking in their ears and expressing contempt for them. They indicated in indecent and shocking gestures what their captives might expect if they should try to escape. Olive and Mary Ann were terrified. They expected to be set upon and killed at any moment by the frantic mob.

Finally, fainting from fear, exhaustion, and hunger, they were shoved rudely into a *wickiup*, where they were permitted to sleep until they awakened the next morning. When they opened their eyes, they were confronted by two old women and an old man. They would soon learn that these people were their owners and they were to be their slaves. They were informed, by gestures, that the old man was the chief of the tribe. He was not called "chief," as the Tontos did not respect authority. However, because he was old, they considered him wise and deferred to his judgment when a decision had to be made. He owned more horses than all of the others combined, a status symbol among Indians. It was expected that all contraband was to be turned over to him and he would distribute it in an equitable manner. Therefore, Olive and Mary Ann became his property, to be disposed of as he saw fit. The two women were his wives and had borne his children, all of whom were adults now.

The tribe consisted of about three hundred, living in filth and degradation. Olive would later learn that this tribe was a rebel group that had seceded from the older and larger tribe of Apaches located in another region of the New Mexico Territory. Dissention had occurred because the rebels were opposed to perceived restraints imposed upon them by the Catholic missionaries and what they considered to be acquiescence to white man's rule by the Apache chiefs. They had resolved upon emancipation and had journeyed to the wild vastness of the northern mountains, where they had established a home. The old tribe had since given them the name "Tonto (crazy) Apaches," an appellation signifying their unruliness as well as their roving, piratical habits. The Tontos asserted that the old tribe was much more corrupt than themselves and that they would soon be destroyed by the whites.

There has always been some confusion concerning which tribe murdered the Oatman family and captured Olive and Mary Ann. Some say it was the Tonto Apaches, while others say the Yavapai were the culprits. The truth of the matter is that the two tribes had been intermingling and intermarrying for many years, and there really was very little distinction between them. Therefore, it could have been one or the other or a combination of both.

Lorenzo Oatman, 1857

Chapter XI
Lorenzo

For what seemed an eternity, Lorenzo lay face down, bleeding from his nose, ears, and head. He appeared to be dead, but was not. He was able to hear everything. After he was struck, he fell to the ground and lay still. He heard the sounds of the clubs crushing the heads of his loved ones. He heard their screams and dying moans. He heard the wild laughter and whoops of the Apaches as they went about their bloody work. Then there were the sounds of the Indians looting the wagon, tearing off the wheels and the covering, and pushing the skeletal remains over the side of the embankment. Then, two of the Indians rolled him over with their feet. They rifled his pockets and took off his shoes and hat. Then they grabbed his feet and dragged him a short distance, leaving him for dead. He heard Olive and Mary Ann crying and pleading with the savages. He heard the mocking laughter of the Apaches as they led the girls away. Then, mercifully, there was nothing as consciousness slipped into darkness.

When he awoke, he was unable to see. He rubbed his eyes to remove the dried blood which had clotted on his eyelids, sealing them shut. The sun beat down upon him. His head was wracked with pain. He looked down at his torn and blood-soaked clothes. He felt his head and found his scalp torn across the top. He made an effort to get up and succeeded in rising to his hands and knees. He was at the foot of a steep, rugged declivity of rocks and did not know whether he had fallen or been thrown there by the Indians. In looking up at the rocks on the embankment above him, he was able to determine his path of descent from the mesa above by the trail of blood on the rocks.

He was aware of his murdered parents, brothers, and sisters on the mesa above him, but could not bring himself to look at them. He determined that the horrible tragedy had occurred the day before. He thought about his sisters being led away by their heathen captors to suffer a thousand deaths. He felt that his brain was loose in his head, and he frantically pressed his head tightly with his hands to keep it from bursting out of his skull. In a state of partial delirium, he imagined himself back in Illinois, surrounded by his playmates in the little schoolyard. He could hear their voices.

"Lorenzo, where are you going? Why are you leaving? Don't you like it here?"

He saw himself, pitying them that they were denied the adventure of an exciting trip across the plains. He remembered the hour of departure, when relatives and friends came to see them off, still trying to persuade them to desist from so hazardous a journey.

Now he saw the wisdom of their counsel. Here he was, a boy of fourteen, the mangled remains of his parents lying nearby, his scalp torn open, covered with blood, alone in a barren, inhospitable land.

Delirium overcame him again. When he awoke, it was with determination to walk or crawl out of this place. He started out, partly standing, partly crouching, climbing slowly up the rock-strewn side of the table land above him. As he approached the top, having crawled almost fifty feet, he came in sight of the wagon wreck. Boxes, open and broken, were strewn about. White feathers from his mother's cherished mattress covered the ground around the wagon. He could not bear to look at the bodies of his loved ones. He turned away and began to crawl toward the east. Soon, he found himself at the slope leading down to the ford of the Gila, where he saw the wagon track they had made the day before. The hot sun aggravated his fever to the boiling point.

He crossed the river, scooping up small handfuls of water to slake his thirst, and stumbled on for a mile or so, where he lay down to rest in the shade of a small bush. Faint as he was with loss of blood and a raging headache, the images of the massacre encroached relentlessly on his consciousness. The dying groans of his beloved family, interspersed with the fiendish laughter of their murderers and the sickening thud of the war clubs, haunted him. Then he would remember the convulsive sobs of little Mary Ann. Exhausted, he slept for three hours.

When he awoke, the sun was behind the western hills. He felt refreshed, but thirsty. He found a sturdy stick, which he used as a cane to help him stay upright. He traveled on, resting only two or three times during the entire night. By daybreak, he had gone about fifteen miles.

About eleven o'clock, he came to a pool of standing water. He lay down and drank from it, though it was warm and muddy. As soon as he had satisfied his thirst, he fell asleep. He awoke partially delirious. Again, he imagined that his brain was trying to jump out of his head, and he pressed his hands to his head to prevent it from happening. By mid-afternoon, he had proceeded about ten miles when he suddenly became faint and fell to the ground. He was, at the time, upon a high table land, sandy and barren. He was soon unconscious.

Late in the afternoon, he was awakened by what he thought was the barking of dogs. In a few moments, he was surrounded by a pack of grey wolves. He was lying in the sun, faint from the heat. He struggled to get to a small tree nearby, but could not. They were now near enough for him to almost touch them.

They were snarling, sniffing, and growling, as if deciding which would be the first to plunge his teeth into his flesh. He summoned all his strength and sprang to his feet, and raising a yell, he struck the nearest one with his hand. The wolf jumped back, and the rest hesitated. This was the first sound Lorenzo had made since the massacre.

He picked up a stone and hurled it at them. They retreated a short distance and then turned and, facing Lorenzo, set up a hideous, doleful howling. It rang out on the still evening air and echoed from crag to crag, sending waves of loneliness and dread through Lorenzo. He tried to scatter them by throwing stones, but they were tenacious. Lorenzo kept walking, and his pursuers followed. The sun had now reached the horizon. He kept himself armed with rocks and occasionally hurled one at the more insolent members of the pack. At times, they would set up one of their wild concerts and grow furious at Lorenzo's retreating body.

It was now dark, and Lorenzo was becoming weak with hunger and thirst. He feared he would collapse and be devoured by these beasts. Late in the evening, they halted and were soon away. Before midnight, the last of their wild yells had died upon the distant hills to the north. The cool night relieved the pain in his head, but he was compelled to maintain a pace much beyond his physical strength to prevent suffering from the cold. He traveled nearly all night. He fell into a troubled sleep toward dawn, dreaming of Indians, bloodshed, his sisters being put to death by slow torture, and that his turn was coming soon.

When he awoke, he scarcely had the strength to move a muscle. He seriously contemplated eating the flesh of his arm to satisfy his hunger. He felt he could not make it to Pimole and that perhaps it would be better to just lie there and die. In spite of these hopeless thoughts, he roused himself and started out. About noon, he was passing through a dark canyon with water dripping from the rocks above. He was able to catch some of the dripping water in his mouth to assuage his thirst. He was about to turn a corner when two red-shirted Maricopa Indians, mounted upon fine American horses, appeared. They drew their bows, pointing their arrows at him.

Lorenzo raised his hand.

"Don't shoot!" he said in Spanish.

They dropped their bows and rode up to him. Lorenzo recognized one of them as an Indian he had been friendly with at the Pimole Village. They looked at him closely for a minute. His friend finally recognized him, despite his disfiguring injuries. He dismounted, strode toward Lorenzo, and embraced him with every expression of pity and sympathy Lorenzo might have expected from one of his own race. He took Lorenzo's hand and asked him what had happened. Lorenzo told them of his family's fate. They took him to a nearby tree and laid him upon their blankets. They took from their saddle a piece of their ash-baked bread and a gourd of water. Lorenzo ate the bread. Fortunately, they did not offer more, or he might have died from overeating, starving as he was. They hung the gourd within his reach and promised to return and take him to Pimole when they had completed their mission.

After sleeping a short time, Lorenzo awoke and, reluctant to wait for the Maricopas' return, he laid the blankets to one side and began to walk again. It was now evening, and the cool night refreshed him. However, he soon became weary, his body wracked with pain. He traveled most of the night, though he was lonely and frightened.

When the fourth morning finally dawned, Lorenzo felt a new optimism. He walked faster, staggering as he went. He was compelled to rest oftener than usual. He knew he could not hold out much longer. His head was inflamed, and in places, his scalp was putrid with infection.

About mid-afternoon, he could go no further and crawled under a shrub to sleep. He slept two or three hours. When he awoke, he prayed out loud, "Oh, God, if I could get something to eat and someone to dress my wounds, I might live."

He now wanted to sleep constantly, but resisted the urge. While sitting there in the shade of the little shrub, trying to muster the strength to rise and walk, he looked down on a long, winding valley below and plainly saw moving objects on the trail. He was sure they were Indians and, for a moment, contemplated killing himself.

For almost an hour, he watched the objects approach until, all at once, they rose up over a small hill. Two white covered wagons! What a sight that was! Lorenzo was so overcome by elation that he fainted and only awoke when he heard a human voice. He opened his eyes to see two covered wagons halted close by and Robert Kelly walking toward him. Lorenzo recognized him at once, but several moments elapsed before Robert knew who this shoeless, hatless, dried-blood-covered boy was.

Chapter XII
Back to Pimole

"My God, Lorenzo, in the name of heaven, what has happened?" Robert cried.

Lorenzo was so overcome, he could not speak. The tears flowed freely down his face. When he regained his composure, he related the story of the massacre and his fear that the Indians had taken Olive and Mary Ann. By this time, John Kelly and the Wilders had left their wagons and stood there staring at Lorenzo in disbelief. They could not speak.

Mrs. Wilder wept and sobbed aloud, begging him to desist from giving them more truth than they could bear. Robert was visibly shaken by the realization that he might never see Olive again and that she might be suffering at the hands of her captors. Tears welled up in his eyes as he carefully picked Lorenzo up and carried him to the Wilders' wagon, where Mrs. Wilder made him comfortable on a mattress in the wagon bed. As Robert walked back to his wagon to join his brother, he clenched his fists in helpless frustration.

They decided immediately to curtail their journey and not venture forth with so small a company and risk a fate similar to the Oatmans'. Mr. Wilder gave Lorenzo some bread and milk, which he gratefully ate. They traveled a few miles back toward Pimole and camped. Lorenzo received every attention and kindness that could be bestowed upon him. They camped near a cool, clear spring, where Lorenzo's wounds were cleaned and his bruised body was bathed.

They were safe at Pimole before nightfall of the following day. When the Pimas learned what had happened, they charged it to the Yumas, as a deadly hostility burned between the two tribes. Willard Wilder and the Kellys resolved to proceed immediately to the place of the massacre and bury the dead.

Early the following day, with two Mexicans and several Pima Indians, they started. They returned after three days. Willard Wilder went straight to the small shelter where his wife sat watching over Lorenzo. He asked her to step outside so that Lorenzo would not hear him.

"We found the mutilated bodies of six persons, two adults and four children. We buried them the best we could. No way to dig graves in that hard, sun-baked ground, so we piled rocks on top of the bodies to protect them from animals."

"You did the best you could, Willard."

"We were able to identify all of the bodies, except for Olive and Mary Ann."

"Oh, God, Willard! It would have been a mercy to Lorenzo if they had found their bodies along with the others. Now he has to live in constant torment, knowing that his sisters are living among those murdering savages, subjected to a barbarous captivity, or death by torture. It's horrible." She was crying and wiping her face with her apron.

"We had to restrain Robert at the massacre site. He became so distraught that he tried to enlist some of the men to ride out with him to search for Olive and Mary Ann. John and I finally convinced him that it would be foolhardy. We don't know where the Indians took the girls, and if, by some miracle, they were to find the place, they would be outnumbered, and the Indians might kill the girls to prevent their rescue."

"I was afraid of that. I saw the way he looked at Olive. He was smitten with her."

"He finally admitted it was hopeless, but I don't think he'll ever get over it. John says Robert talked about marrying Olive someday. He must be going through hell right now."

Willard Wilder was right. Robert would continue to have nightmares of her fate at the hands of the Indians.

The two Maricopas that had met Lorenzo along the trail returned to the Pimole village with bolts of calico and some clothing they had found at the massacre site. Wilder and Kelly took these things from them and sold them to the Pimas and Maricopas. Later, Mormon missionaries would see these things and assume that the Maricopas had murdered the Oatmans. They later reported this to Major Heintzelman at Fort Yuma, and he made mention of it in his Fort Yuma log entry dated May 15, 1851. Based on the Mormons' report, Heintzelman made the mistaken assumption that the Maricopas had murdered the Oatmans.

For a week, Lorenzo was dangerously ill, but with the kind attention and nursing given to him by Mrs.Wilder and a few Pima Indian women, he began to revive. Willard Wilder sent a Pima runner to Tukjon with a letter for the four families that had remained there, informing them of the Oatman massacre, the kidnapping of Olive and Mary Ann, and the survival of Lorenzo.

Now they waited for some travelers heading west to accompany them to California. When they had been there for two weeks, seven men riding six mules arrived at Pimole. They related their story to the Wilders and Kellys.

"We're American soldiers, but we deserted our post in the New Mexico mountains. We were in such a hurry to get away that we lost one of our mules. We had to take turns walking while the others rode." At this, they all laughed.

"We have two wagons and a boy who was part of a family killed by Apaches. He was badly beaten and left for dead. We need to get him to the doctor at Fort Yuma. Is it all right if we travel with you?" Willard Wilder asked.

"Sure, but we'll have to leave you before we get to the fort. You can understand why."

"Yes, of course. When will you be ready to leave?"

"If we can get some grub and a good night's sleep, we can leave tomorrow morning. How about it, boys?"

The deserters nodded their agreement, and Willard went to tell the others the good news.

They were soon on the road again. On the sixth day, they reached the place of the massacre. It was more than Lorenzo could bear. He could hear the echo of those hellish war whoops reverberating among the mountain cliffs. He relived those awful moments, the terrible groans of his dying family. This was haunted ground. As he lay in the back of the Wilders' wagon, Mrs. Wilder pressed a cool cloth to his forehead.

"Don't think about it, Lorenzo," she said.

With the exception of about eighteen miles of desert, they had a comfortable week of travel and arrived at Fort Yuma on March 27, 1851. Lorenzo was still in serious condition, but his mental suffering was worse than his physical pain.

Chapter XIII
Fort Yuma

FORT YUMA

As they waited their turn for the ferry on what is now the Arizona side but at that time was known as the New Mexico Territory, the landing bustled with activity. They took in the welcome sight of Fort Yuma on the opposite bank of the river. It was situated on a bluff overlooking the Colorado. Although the term *fort* would tend to indicate an impressive fortification, fully equipped to fight off an enemy attack, it was merely an assortment of tents and poorly constructed shacks. As disappointing as it was, it appeared to the grateful emigrants as a shining citadel upon the hill, a beacon of safety in this savage country.

It had been hastily erected on the site of a former Catholic mission founded in 1779 by Father Garces, a Spanish priest. In 1781, the Yuma Indians had become angry with the Spanish and had massacred all of the Spaniards in the area, including Father Garces and his guide, Sebastian. The Yumas later felt remorse for murdering the priest, who had been a friend to them, and buried him and Sebastian with respect.

When it was the Wilders' and the Kellys' turn to board the ferry, they drove their wagons and animals onto the sturdy barges, which were then hauled to the other side of the river by rope tows. When they drove the teams off of the ferry and onto land, Willard Wilder turned to Lorenzo, who was resting in the bed of the of the wagon, and shouted, "Lorenzo, we are now in California."

In spite of his pain, Lorenzo smiled and said, "Hallelujah. Thank the Lord!"

At the fort, Lorenzo was taken to the infirmary, where he was given the best medical care possible by Dr. Henry S. Hewitt, the fort physician. The Wilders and the Kellys learned from Dr.Hewitt that Dr. Le Conte had arrived almost as soon as he would have if his horse had not been stolen. He had gone immediately to the fort commander, Brevet Major Samuel Peter Heintzelman, with the letter written by Royce Oatman.

Heintzelman had looked up when Le Conte entered his office.

"Well, well, if it isn't Dr. Bugs," he said, sarcastically referring to Le Conte's profession as an entomologist.

Dr. Le Conte ignored Heintzelman's deprecating remark. He took Royce Oatman's letter from his breast pocket and handed it to Heintzelman.

Heintzelman glanced at the letter and said, "I am extremely short-handed at the moment and cannot spare any men to send to his aid."

Dr. Le Conte shuffled his feet and cleared his throat.

"But, as fort commander, you are sworn to protect the emigrants."

"I am in no position to protect anyone at the moment."

Frustrated, Dr. Le Conte turned and stomped out of the office. There were a number of brave men at the fort who volunteered to go to the Oatmans' assistance, but permission could not be obtained from Heintzelman.

After several days, Heintzelman reluctantly sent two men, who rode east toward Pimole until they came to the scene of the massacre. Sick at heart and angry over the callous neglect of their commander, whose prompt action might have saved this poor family, or at least prevented the capture of the two girls, they headed back to the fort. They reported their findings to Major Heintzelman, including the fact that the massacre took place on the south side of the Gila River, which was, at that time, Mexican territory.[2]

Heintzelman would later use this as an excuse for not sending troops out as soon as Dr. Le Conte gave him Oatman's letter. He also stated lack of personnel as a reason for his inaction. However, according to Heintzelman's own entry in the Fort Yuma log, Le Conte gave him Oatman's letter on February 21, 1851, and, according to the records of the California Military Museum in Sacramento, California, troop levels at Fort Yuma were not reduced until June 1851, when the army virtually abandoned the post, with the exception of twelve soldiers who remained at the fort to guard the ferry crossing.

It was common knowledge at the fort that Heinzelman was preoccupied with his own personal and business interests. He was considered a "fussy little man." He was part-owner of the ferry company which was the only way people and goods could be transported across the Colorado River from New Mexico territory to Fort Yuma and California. The high tolls collected for the ferry, the subject of many complaints from emigrants, provided him with a substantial income.

---

[2] At the time of the massacre, the Gadsden Purchase had not yet been signed. It went into effect in 1853, two years later. It included 29,670 square miles of the region south of the Gila River,and west of the Rio Grande, which was purchased from Mexico by the United States for $10 million (about 53 cents an acre). The purchase was initiated for the purpose of providing for construction of a southern route for a transcontinental railroad, and is now known as southern Arizona and New Mexico.

His daily entries In the Fort Yuma log reveal much about Heintzelman's character. His preoccupation with food is evident in the fact that he describes what he had for dinner each night. One entry in particular is of interest. It states that several flats of strawberries had been obtained by the fort purser and placed in the storeroom. He was looking forward to having fresh strawberries for dessert that evening, and he became incensed when informed that the strawberries had vanished from the commissary. He makes a great fuss over the matter, threatening to apprehend the thief and subject him to a court martial.

BREVET MAJOR SAMUEL P. HEINTZELMAN

On March 27, 1851, as soon as they had left Lorenzo in the care of Dr. Hewitt, Willard Wilder and the Kelly brothers went to see Commander Heintzelman. They entered his office and stood waiting for him to finish writing. He sat behind a large, distressed mahogany desk. His chair was also mahogany and upholstered in Mexican leather. A few vivid paintings of famous battles hung upon the white-plastered adobe walls.

He looked up with heavy-lidded eyes which gave him a bored expression.

"Gentlemen, what can I do for you?" he said.

"Sir, we are here to ask your assistance in organizing a search party to rescue two young girls captured by the Indians who murdered their family on the Gila River," said Willard Wilder.

"Are you referring to the Oatman family?"

"Yes, sir, I am."

"I sent two men out to assist them, but it was too late. They were all dead."

"Not all, sir. Besides the captured girls, there was one survivor, Lorenzo Oatman, a boy of fifteen. He was clubbed over the head and left for dead, but managed to walk fifteen miles in three days when we found him on the Gila trail. We took him back to Pimole, where we joined six men heading west and traveled here with them. Lorenzo is now in your dispensary under the care of Dr. Hewitt."

"Remarkable. I would like to speak to him when he's up to it. Perhaps he can give me a firsthand account of the massacre and who the perpetrators were. We need to make a full report. As I understand it, this incident occurred south of the Gila River in Mexican territory. I cannot send troops there."

"But, sir, surely you have a duty to protect two helpless little girls, American citizens being held captive by a hostile Indian tribe."

"Sir, do not tell me what my duties are. I know what I can and cannot do."

Willard Wilder was frustrated. He felt they had hit a brick wall with Heintzelman, but did not want to antagonize him further.

"Thank you for your time, Commander," he said and turned to leave.

The Kellys followed him, muttering, "Thank you, sir."

Once outside, Robert broke down. He had managed to control his emotions, feeling certain that help would be forthcoming from Fort Yuma. Now Heintzelman had dashed his hopes, and he felt powerless and frustrated.

"Damned pompous little bureaucrat!" he muttered, his fists clamped tensely at his sides. "I'll get some men together and go myself."

He found soldiers at the fort who were ready and willing, but not able. Several soldiers petitioned Major Heintzelman to let them go on a search detail, but again, Heintzelman refused permission.

Robert was now anxious to move on to California, where he intended to petition a newspaper to take up the cause. However, he and John stayed on at the fort for a few more weeks when they were offered work building a boat from cottonwood, the only timber available in the area. He planned to use his earnings to finance a rescue mission.

The Wilders and the Kellys resumed their westward journey with another wagon train that had stopped at the fort. Dr. Hewitt offered to take care of Lorenzo until such time as family members could be located.

Some excerpts from the 1851 Fort Yuma log, as entered by Brevet Major Heintzelman, reveal some of his thoughts on the matter of the Oatman massacre and the subsequent kidnapping of Olive and Mary Ann.

Friday, February 21: "Dr. Le Conte brought a letter from an emigrant (Royce Oatman) asking for four horses."

Saturday, March 8: "Two soldiers sent to search for distressed emigrants. They went to the massacre scene. Kelly and W. Wilder had already gathered up the remains and piled stones on them."

Note: Heintzelman does not mention that, while at Pimole, the two soldiers learned of the capture of the Oatman sisters and searched for them until their provisions were exhausted. They returned to the fort and asked Major Heintzelman for more men and provisions so they could conduct a more thorough search. Their request was ignored.

Sunday, March 9: "Captain Davidson is urging me to send out a party to see about the emigrants (Oatmans) and go as far as the Pimas (Pima village). Dr. Le Conte refuses to accompany them, as they (the Oatmans) were murdered by Indians and two young women carried off as captives."

March 27: "Emigrants (Wilders and Kellys) arrive with Lorenzo Oatman." (There is no mention of his conversation with Willard Wilder and the Kelly brothers regarding a search for Olive and Mary Ann.)

March 31: "Olive Oatman was thirteen; Mary Ann was eight." (Olive was fourteen.)

May 15: "Mormon missionaries reported having seen some of the Oatmans' clothing in the Pima village. When the Mormons recognized it, the Indians took it away. They were offering it for sale. There is no doubt now: the Maricopas were the murderers."

September 29: "The Pimas have accused the Apaches of murdering the Oatmans."

If may be argued that if Heintzelman had sent out a contingent of soldiers immediately upon receipt of Royce Oatman's letter on February 21, 1851, they might have been able to track the Apache murderers and their captives. Since they had horses and the Indians were on foot, slowed down by their captives, the soldiers might have been able to overtake them before they reached the Apache village.

Dr. Hewitt wrote a letter to the *San Francisco Alta Californian,* criticizing Heintzelman for not doing enough for the Oatmans. He stated that Heintzelman was derelict in his duty to protect the emigrants. He also wrote to Heintzelman's superiors, leveling the same charges.

On May 17, 1851, Dr. Le Conte had a letter published in the *San Francisco Herald,* giving his version of the murder of the Oatman family and of Major Heintzelman's failure to act upon receipt of Royce Oatman's letter asking for help.

When Heintzelman read Hewitt's letter in the *Alta Californian,* he countered in a letter to the *Alta Californian* dated July 14, 1851. In it, he argued that the incident had occurred in Mexican territory, and the U.S. Army had no business sending troops into Mexican territory. He further stated that he had only twelve men stationed at Fort Yuma at the time and could not spare them. (This was untrue. There was a full complement of men at the fort until early June of 1851, when all but twelve left for San Diego.) Furthermore, he accused Dr. Hewitt and Dr. Le Conte of being "disgruntled because I had refused them a military escort for their prospecting expedition."

Heintzelman's superiors apparently accepted his explanation, as there is no record of a reprimand. He was transferred out of Fort Yuma and was replaced by Major George C. Thomas. Major Thomas was transferred to Texas in 1855 and was replaced by Brevet Lieutenant Martin Burke. Heintzelman's transfer out of Fort Yuma removed him from his preoccupation with the ferry business, and it is not known if he continued to have a financial interest in it.

After reviewing all the documents regarding this matter, Hubert Howe Bancroft, a noted historian and author, concluded that Heintzelman's excuses for not taking action were insufficient.

While they were at Fort Yuma, the Wilders and the Kellys had plenty of time to observe the area that James Brewster had described in such glowing terms as "the land of Bashan, the earthy Eden, with rich bottomlands, good stands of timber, and friendly Indians." They were disappointed, but not surprised, as they had lost faith in Brewster months ago. In truth, it was the hottest and driest place in the country, with rocks outnumbering the few cottonwoods that stood along the riverbanks.

Mrs. Wilder sent the following letter to her father:

"It seems that it never rains here to do any good or hurt. The ferrymen say they have been here for ten months and it has not rained enough to wet their shirts through.

In consequence of there being no turf, it is very dusty, as the wind blows two days out of seven; and when the wind does not blow, about three o'clock, midges (gnats) bite unmercifully."

Chapter XIV
The Families That Stayed Behind

After the Kellys, the Wilders, and the Oatmans had left Tukjon, five other families remained. They planned to stay at least a year to raise grain and cattle. They were the Thompsons, the Brimhalls, the Muteres, the Cheesbroughs, and the Lanes. Toward the end of February 1851, a Pima Indian arrived in their camp with a letter from Willard Wilder informing them of the fate of the Oatmans. The five families were shocked and grief-stricken when they read of the massacre, the survival of Lorenzo, and the capture of Olive and Mary Ann by the murderers. Susan Thompson was inconsolable for several days. She grieved for Lucy, who had been her best friend. She asked her mother, "If there is a God, how could he let a sweet, innocent girl like Lucy be murdered by savages?"

Mrs. Thompson had no answer. She comforted Susan, holding her and patting her back.

"She's with God now. That's the most important thing," she said

They stayed in Tukjon until a sheep herder named John Raines arrived with his partners and three thousand sheep, which they were driving from Mexico to California. Four of the five families decided to travel with the Raines party to Fort Yuma in relative safety. They left Tucson around the fourth week in May 1851. The Cheesbroughs stayed behind in Tukjon.

Only the Thompsons and the Lanes arrived at Fort Yuma with the Raines party. The Brimhalls and the Muteres left the party and headed north to Phoenix, where a new settlement had sprung up.

By the time the Thompsons and the Lanes arrived at Fort Yuma, the Kellys and the Wilders had gone on to California and Lorenzo had gone to San Francisco with Dr. Hewitt. The Raines party did not linger at the fort, as they were under a deadline to deliver the sheep.

Shortly after arriving at Fort Yuma, Mrs. Thompson gave birth to a baby girl. She was named Gila after the river they had followed west to the Colorado. Dr. Hughes, who had succeeded Dr. Hewitt as fort physician, not only delivered the new baby, but he was able to help Mr. Thompson and their young daughter, Lucy, who were quite ill when they arrived at the fort. After a few days' rest, they were well and ready to travel on to California with the Lanes.

In her later writings from El Monte, Susan Thompson said that, although her father had been smitten by gold fever, he never went to the gold country, but opened the Willow Grove Inn at El Monte to serve the many travelers passing that way to the gold fields. One of these travelers was David Lewis, an emigrant from New York. In October of 1853, Susan left the Willow Grove Inn as David Lewis' bride.

After a long silence, *The Olive Branch,* volume 4, number 2, of September,1851, contains a letter from Mrs. Wilder written from California, dated May 16,1851. It reads, in part, as follows:

> On November 9th, 1850, Oatman and part of the company went ahead, leaving the Muteres, the Kellys, and us behind. He drove so long the oxen did not have time to eat, and we were afraid our cattle would not be able to take us through, so we let them go ahead. We passed them before we got to Santa Cruz. After we passed them, Oatman left Brimhall and Cheesbrough. On the 18th of February, 1851, we started with the Kellys (from Pimole), and on the 20th (22nd) we met Oatman's oldest son, Lorenzo, fifteen years of age. He was tired, hungry, bruised, and bloody. He said he supposed that his people were all killed.
> Willard (Wilder) and Robert Kelly went down to Oatman's wagon, a distance of seventy-five miles, to bury the dead and see what was there. Oatman had seven children, and only five could be found. It is supposed that the Indians carried off two girls, one fourteen and the other eight years old.

Chapter XV
Captivity Among the Apaches

The Tonto Apaches were a mangy lot. Olive was appalled by their lack of modesty. In good weather, the men wore nothing but breechcloths. The women wore skirts made from bark and nothing else. They subsisted principally on deer, quail, and rabbit, with occasional roots from the ground. They would hunt only when faced with starvation. At times, game in the immediate area was scarce, but, unless faced with starvation, they were too lazy to travel to the mountains and valleys where game was plentiful. During their captivity among the Apache, Olive and Mary Ann experienced many entire days when they were not given a scrap of food.

Women were not allowed to eat meat, and captives were allowed a morsel only when unusual abundance chanced to arrive. This they had to share with the dogs. Their meat was boiled with water in a *tusquin* (clay kettle), and this meat-mush, or soup, was their main staple of food. If this was in short supply, it was supplemented with roots.

When a hunter returned with game, he was surrounded by hungry crowds ready to pounce and devour it like wolves. The bits and leavings were tossed to the captives, whom the Indians called *Onatas*. They would taunt Olive and Mary Ann, saying, "You *Onatas* have been fed too well. We will teach you to live on little."

Considering that the mainstay of their diet was game, denying meat to women had the effect of dooming them to starvation. Females, especially young females, were permitted to eat meat only when necessary to prevent starving to death. Their own female children frequently died, and those who lived, old and young, were generally sickly and dwarfish. Several times, Olive and Mary Ann were brought to the brink of death before the males would waive their superstitions and give them a saving morsel of meat. In her lecture notes, Olive wrote: "These Apaches were not industrious. They did not raise crops. They knew nothing about cultivating the soil, even though they had soil that might have produced."

It was amazing to Olive and Mary Ann how little it took to keep them alive, yet they were capable of great strength and endurance. Olive would later write, "They ate worms, grasshoppers, snakes, all flesh, and were living proof of the expression 'you are what you eat.' These stout, robust, lazy lumps of degraded humanity would lounge in the sun or by the bubbling spring or in the shade of the mountains, oblivious to the consequences their inaction had on the tribe."

Women were the laborers and burden bearers. During their captivity, Olive and Mary Ann served under these enslaved women, who drove them mercilessly and took delight in whipping them. Their demands were made in the most insulting and taunting manner, indicative of their hatred of the white race. Children, some younger than Olive and Mary Ann, were taskmasters. The captives were required to tend to their every whimper with promptness, or suffer a severe beating.

For some time after coming among them, Mary Ann was very ill. The fatigue and the cruelties of the journey and everyday life nearly cost her life. Yet, with all her weakness, sickness, and despair, they treated her like a dog. Mary Ann would often say to Olive, "I will starve unless I can get something more to eat."

Occasionally, when she became too disabled, they allowed her a respite from some menial daily task. As they gathered roots for their lazy captors, they would eat some themselves. In this way, they managed to survive, but just barely.

Olive learned to hide whenever a man approached her. She had discovered a certain root which produced a yellow stain when rubbed on the skin. She carried a few in her apron pocket and applied it liberally to her arms and face on those occasions when there was no place to hide. She would point to her yellow skin and say "sick" in the Apache language. This usually had the immediate effect of suppressing desire, as it was well known among the Indian tribes that white people sometimes carried diseases for which the Indians had no defense. Moreover, the Tontos had no witch doctors to "purify" the captives or cure disease. The witch doctors had remained with the old Apache tribe.

This ruse worked most of the time, but occasionally it did not. On those few occasions when resistance was hopeless, she would be forced to submit or suffer the consequences. She became adept at separating her spirit from her body. She rationalized that whatever terrible things might be happening to her body, her soul would rise above it and endure. Afterward. she would pray that she would not become pregnant. There was nothing to fear from the old chief, as he was impotent. He had approached her many times, thinking her youth would restore his virility, but he was unable to perform.

She was thankful that Mary Ann was not molested. The men seemed to regard her as a delicate little doll. They would often tousle her blonde curls and pretend to scalp her, which frightened Mary Ann and produced gales of laughter from the men.

Worse than the physical deprivation they suffered at the hands of their captors was the mental anguish, fear of the future. They lived at the pleasure of the tribe. The slightest infraction of their rules could incur their wrath and bring heavy punishment, even death. As a means of survival, they soon learned the Apache language.

Mary Ann would often come to Olive, sobbing over the maltreatment that had met her good intentions to please.

"How long must we stay here, Olive? Can we ever get away? Do you think they will kill us?"

"I see no chance for escape, Mary Ann. If we attempt it and fail, they will most certainly kill us, and in a most horrible and painful way. We must pray and wait, in submission, for our lot. God will help us endure."

It was their custom to pray every day when they were alone together. If an opportunity did not present itself during the day, they would pray when they laid their heads down on their sand beds at night.

Sometimes, they would sing hymns when they were sent long distances to gather water and wood for the comfort of lazy men. Prayer and singing sustained them in those long, dark days. There was no beauty in this land. The days were hot and dry and the nights cold and permeated with the howls of coyotes.

As depressing as their situation was, they were not without hope. They would sometimes catch snatches of their captors' conversations concerning trips to some region of the whites. Occasionally, they gained some knowledge of their location.

When Olive and Mary Ann had been among the Apaches for several months, they began to notice a change in their captors' attitude. They became more lenient and merciful, especially to Mary Ann. She had met their abuse with a patience and fortitude beyond her years. This spirit eventually had its effect on the Indians, especially the females connected with the household of the chief.

The girls plainly saw signs of kindness and interest exhibited toward them. After a few months, the girls were able to converse with them in their language. They asked the girls about their ages, their former place of residence, how many white people there were, how far the big oceans extended, and if the whites possessed the other big world on the east side of the Atlantic. They were curious to know if there were any Indians there. They were particularly interested in the number of *Americanos,* a term learned from the Mexicans.

When Olive told them of the number of whites and of their rapid increase, they appeared incredulous. Some would become angry and accuse Olive of lying. They wanted to know how women were treated and if a man was allowed more than one wife. They were particularly interested in learning how the white man lived and what contributed to the success and increase of the whites.

Olive told them of the many occupations and industries of the whites. She related some facts she had learned in school: that the earth rotated on its axis every twenty-four hours and traveled around the sun every year and that the white man had calculated the distance to far-off stars and planets. They found this incredible and shouted, "You are a big liar, just like all the *Americanos.*"

However, Olive and Mary Ann could ascertain from the heated discussions they engaged in afterwards that they did not totally disbelieve everything Olive told them.

These Apaches sincerely believed that an evil spirit reigned among the whites and that he was leading them on to destruction. They insisted that there were scarcely any whites that could be trusted, but that they had evil assistance that made them powerful.

This tribe had no system of religion or morality. They were given to humor and fun, but it quickly descended to low obscenity and meanness. They were contemptuous of anyone who would complain under torture or suffering. They believed that a person who could not endure suffering without complaining was not fit to live. They asked the girls if they wanted to get away and tried to extract from them any feeling about their captivity. Olive and Mary Ann soon learned not to express discontent, as this elicited new tasks and punishments.

Isolated as they were, the Tontos had established trading relations with the Mojaves, a tribe numbering about twelve hundred and located about three hundred miles to the northwest. The Mojaves made an expedition once a year, sometimes oftener, to the Apaches in small groups, bringing with them vegetables, grain, and other agricultural products which they would exchange with the Apaches for animal skins and whatever other articles the Apaches might be interested in trading.

Late in the autumn of 1851, a large company of Mojaves arrived at the Apache camp on a trading expedition. This was the first time Olive and Mary Ann had seen these superior Indians. During their stay, Olive and May Ann overheard conversations indicating that the Apaches were contemplating the exchange of the two white captives for vegetables and other edibles. However, nothing came of it, and the Mojaves soon departed. Olive and Mary Ann resumed their lives of drudgery.

Months passed, and the girls continued to work from dawn to dusk to please their masters. But since the coming of these Mojaves, the Apaches spent hours at a time conversing about the possibility of selling Olive and Mary Ann to them. Some argued that having to maintain constant vigilance over the captives to prevent their possible escape was extremely taxing. They feared that, if they were to escape, Olive and Mary Ann might return to their own people and tell the tale of their sufferings at the hands of the Apaches and thus bring down the vengeance of the whites upon them. Selling the captives to the Mojaves, as remote and inaccessible as they were, would insure that the captives could not escape.

Chapter XVI
New Owners

A year after they had been taken captive, Olive and Mary Ann sat on a small mound a short distance from the Apache village. It was a pleasant day, and, with their root baskets side by side on the ground between them, Olive and Mary Ann spoke of all that had happened to them during the past year. They spoke about their dead parents and their dead brothers and sisters. They spoke of their pain and suffering at the hands of their captors. Then Mary Ann said, "Oh, Olive, I believe they will sell us. I heard the chief say something about our going to the Mojaves and that they would soon come for us. From what I saw of them, I think they know more and live better than these miserable Apaches."

"Perhaps we have only seen their good side. They might treat us worse than the Apaches," said Olive.

"That would be impossible, unless they kill us. If we cannot escape, the sooner, the better. We could start tonight, Olive. I know I could go the distance," said Mary Ann.

"But where shall we go? We traveled by night and do not know the way. These Indians have their trails through the mountains. They could easily head us off. They travel in small bands to hunt down helpless travelers to rob and kill. They would find us and bring us back here."

"Olive, haven't you always said if it were not for a faint hope of getting away, and your concern for me, you would rather die than live like this? We both know they intend to sell us to the Mojaves and we will have to travel three hundred miles to their village. I could never live through it. My cough grows more severe each night. Ma always said her Mary Ann would die of consumption."

Olive looked at Mary Ann with pity. She saw how her eyes seemed to sink deeper into her head and how spare and pale her cheeks were.

"Mary Ann, if you are afraid that you would perish in traveling to the Mojave country, how could you stand traveling day and night among the hills, away from the trail, for a week, perhaps a month, living on roots?"

"Roots are about all we get now, and I would rather live on them trying to get away than staying here and being driven like oxen again for three hundred miles."

Mary Ann was about to continue when Olive, seeing an Apache close by, hushed her. They busied themselves digging roots.

When they returned to the village, a general commotion prevailed.

Several Indians were approaching. The party consisted of five men and a young woman. Two of the men rode horses, while the others, including the woman, were on foot.

"Look! They are Mojaves," Mary Ann whispered.

Olive was half-inclined to take advantage of the excitement and carelessness following the Mojaves' arrival to slip away, taking a piece of meat, a few roots, and something to kill herself and Mary Ann with should they be re-captured. It was only out of fear of being caught and tortured that she decided against it.

As the Mojaves descended the slope to the village, roaring, yelling, and dancing prevailed among the Apaches.

Soon after the Mojaves' arrival, two Apache leaders came to Olive and Mary Ann. One spoke.

"The Mojaves have come to take you, according to a contract we made with them on their last visit. They have obtained the approval of Espaniole, the Mojave chief, and he has sent his own daughter to witness his desire to purchase the white captives. The chief has left it to his daughter to make the final decision."

The Mojave chief's daughter was a beautiful, mild, and sympathetic young woman. Her conduct toward Olive and Mary Ann evidenced an intelligence and sweetness of disposition that won their interest at once. She was fluent in the Apache language and could converse with Olive and Mary Ann.

"My name is Tokwa Oa, daughter of Homeseh Awahot, great chief of the Mojaves. He is called 'Espaniole' by his people because he speaks Spanish, which enables us to trade with the Mexicans. We have returned to take you with us out of kindness. We knew of the cruel treatment you were enduring among the Apaches, and we intend to use you well."

Olive and Mary Ann would have been comforted by these words if they had not been familiar with the treachery they had come to expect from the Indians. They saw only gloom in their future, whether they went with the Mojaves or remained with the Apaches.

That evening, there was unrest and unruliness throughout the village. Olive and Mary Ann were confused and apprehensive when they learned that their future was still undecided. There was much dissention among a certain group who were opposed to the sale. As the girls huddled in their little *wickiup,* Mary Ann spoke of her concerns.

"Olive, I'm afraid there are some Apaches who do not want us to go with the Mojaves."

"Yes, they're opposed to the sale. They feel they are losing their slaves and getting nothing in return. The chief and his council are being compensated by the Mojaves, but those who murdered our family and captured us feel they are being cheated."

Olive and Mary Ann were approached by various Apaches in an attempt to draw them out on the subject of their impending sale. One woman, in particular, Toaquin, who had endeavored from the first to ingratiate herself with Olive, sought to make her say that she would rather go with the Mojaves. On several occasions in the past, Toaquin had eavesdropped and borne tales to the chief. Aware of her treachery, Olive gave no indication of her discontent with her life or of any desire to leave. While Olive and Mary Ann sat alone in their little wigwam late at night, Toaquin entered and sat herself down by the fire, smiling and pretending to be interested in their welfare.

"I suppose you are glad you are going to the Mojaves? I always hated them. They will steal, lie, and cheat. Do you think you will get away? Perhaps you do, but these Mojaves are going to sell you to another tribe. If they do not, it will not be long before they kill you. I am very sad because you are going away. I hoped to see you free in a short time, but you will never get back to the whites now. I suppose you will try, will you not?"

Olive was careful in her reply.

"We are captives, and since our parents and all our kindred are dead, it matters little where we are, there or here. We are treated better than we deserve here, and we shall try to behave well, let them treat us as they may. As to getting away, you know it would be foolish for us to try."

At sunrise, after a sleepless night, Olive and Mary Ann were informed by their Apache captors that they must go with the Mojaves. Two horses, a few vegetables, a few pounds of beads, and three blankets was the price paid for them.

As they left the Apache village, those who were opposed to the sale of the captives, including the murderers of the Oatman family, attempted to incite the others to prevent them from leaving. There were those who wanted to tear the captives to pieces and followed them, angrily spitting forth threats and insults. Some laughed, and many of the children who had received care and attention from the captives cried. A general pow-wow rent the air as the captives started upon another three-hundred-mile journey with their new owners.

Chapter XVII
Captivity Among the Mojaves

Olive and Mary Ann were told, at the outset, that they had three hundred and fifty miles to travel, all on foot. The two horses the Mojaves rode in on had been left at the Apache village as part payment for the captives.

Their route was in no way preferable to the one by which the Apache village had been reached. It was now about the first day of March, 1852. Olive and Mary Ann had endured a year of cruelty, barbarity, and hatred in a rugged, rocky country of bare mountains and scarce vegetation. Now they were being hurried along over piles of boulders and gravel beds in rough terrain, not knowing where they were going or what their fate would be.

Olive worried about Mary Ann. She had begun this trip with less strength or fortitude than the one before. She had not gone far before it was plain that she could not keep up this pace. Despite all the appearances of kindness that these Mojaves manifested, they seemed devoid of any compassion for their captives and their inability to perform the tasks which the rough and ready Indians were inured to.

With sore, bleeding feet, Olive and Mary Ann were not able to keep up the rapid pace. After noon on the second day, a small piece of meat was given to them, and this, with the few roots they were allowed to dig, became their sole sustenance for ten days.

On the second day, they were allowed to rest a short time under protest from their captors. After this, they were not compelled to travel more than thirty-five miles in a day. Pieces of skins were furnished for their feet, but not until they had been bruised and mangled. The nights were cool, and, to the captives' surprise, Tokwa Oa showed them kindness throughout the journey by sharing her blankets with them at each camp. The rugged, inhospitable country through which they traveled during those ten days was devoid of any vegetation other than an occasional cactus or sagebrush.

On the eleventh day, about two hours before sunset, they made a steep climb to a precipice, from which they had a panoramic view. Below them lay a narrow valley covered with a carpet of green that stretched a distance of about twenty miles. Protecting the valley on either side were high, irregularly shaped mountains, their foothills clothed in the same bright green. The mountains, with their bald hump-backs and sharp peaks, were treeless and desolate.

The Mojaves became very animated, and it was clear by their lively discussion that they had observed something in the valley below that captured their attention. Olive and Mary Ann followed their gaze and saw gentle columns of smoke rising from the valley floor just a few miles away. Soon, they noticed a large number of huts dotting the valley in every direction. A cluster of these huts huddled into a nook in the hills to the right on the bank of a wide, shining river. A row of cottonwood trees in their spring green splendor lined the banks of the river and followed its zigzag course through the valley.

Mary Ann was ecstatic.

"Here is where they live, Olive. Isn't it a beautiful valley? I would like to live here."

"Maybe you will not want to return to the whites again."

"Oh, yes, there are green grass and fine meadows there, besides good people who would care for us. These Indians only want to make slaves of us."

They were soon escorted into the Mojave Valley and past the low, rude huts of the Mojave Indians. They were greeted with shouts, dance, and song as they passed. The little party maintained a brisk, steady march for the village, followed by unkempt Mojaves and dirty children. Olive wondered how the Mojaves could be so unclean when the proximity of the river provided ample water to bathe in. These Mojaves approached the captives, looked rudely into their faces, fastened their small, deep-set, black eyes upon them, and walked alongside them, whooping and dancing along their path.

Olive and Mary Ann accompanied Tokwa Oa to the chief's house, where they were met with the stares of curious onlookers and an occasional smile from the members of the chief's family. Family members included Tokwa Oa's parents, two married sisters, and their husbands and children. They expressed great joy over the return of Tokwa Oa, though she had been gone just over twenty days. Olive and Mary Ann were surprised by this demonstration of affection. They had never experienced such a show of emotion by Indians.

The chief's house was on a small, but beautiful, elevation crowning the riverbank, with a sweeping view of the valley and the entire village, a portion of which lined each bank of the stream.

The house was set inside a perfect square of about one hundred feet which was outlined by a perfect row of cottonwood trees, their branches interlocking and putting out their new spring foliage. Many of these cottonwood groves were scattered throughout the village, creating an oasis in the otherwise barren region over which the captives had been driven for the past ten days. The soil here along the riverbank seemed rich in contrast to the rocks and burning sands over which they had traveled.

Immediately behind the row of trees surrounding the chief's house was a row of poles, or logs, each about six inches in diameter, set close together with one end firmly implanted in the ground and extending upward about twenty feet, forming an enclosure of about fifty feet.

The three girls entered this enclosure through a door (never shut) and entered a tidy yard planted in grass. Inside of this was still another enclosure of about twenty feet walled by the same kind of fence, only about one-third as high. The walls of the chief's house were about three feet above the height of the outside row, with a ridge for the support of the roof. The roof was a thick mat of limbs and mud. Just inside the door was a small, smoking fire, bare walls, and a dirt floor. A few blankets were scattered about the room.

On entering the house, Tokwa Oa saw a cake roasting in the ashes. She promptly seized it and, dividing it into three parts, gave Olive and Mary Ann a portion. They hungrily devoured the cake and found it surprisingly tasty.

Tokwa Oa had been kind, despite the breakneck pace she and her companions had enforced on the captives. She was intelligent and seemed capable of true sympathy and affection. During their journey, she had told Olive and Mary Ann she was seventeen years old. She was sprightly, jovial, and good-natured. At times, she manifested a deep sympathy for her captives and commiserated with their desolate condition. When told of the massacre of the Oatman family by the Apaches, tears welled up in her eyes, and she touched the hands of Olive and Mary Ann as if to comfort them.

Though she was the daughter of the chief, she was still a woman and had walked the three hundred miles to the Apache village, carrying a roll of blankets, while two healthy, stalwart braves had ridden the two trade horses. Mary Ann could not seem to pronounce *Tokwa Oa* and began to call her Topeka instead. It was a Kansas town they had passed through on their westward journey, and the name had lodged somewhere in Mary Ann's memory. Tokwa Oa did not mind the name Topeka; in fact, she seemed to like it, especially when Mary Ann said it. Just about everything Mary Ann said or did amused Tokwa Oa.

That evening, there was a large gathering of Indians with their brown, stout wives and daughters and swarms of little ones, whose faces and bare limbs were dirty despite the proximity of water. The male members of the tribe were mostly tall, with large heads and broad faces, and of a much more intelligent appearance than the Apaches. The men wore bark breechcloths, and the women, who were short and undernourished, wore short bark skirts, indicating a warm climate and a scarcity of cloth.

Their conduct during that night of wild excitement and celebration was very different from that manifested by the Apaches. That was one of barbarous fiends gloating over their murderous deeds of death and plunder. Here, the Mojaves expressed joy over the return of kindred and the purchase of two foreign captives. Olive and Mary Ann were placed out on the green, and, in the light of a huge, brisk fire, the Mojaves kept up their dancing, singing, jumping, and shouting until just before daybreak.

After they had dispersed, Olive and Mary Ann lay down on a sand bed beneath a thin blanket and conversed in low whispers.

"My feet are bleeding and worn, in some places, to the bone. My arms and legs ache," said Mary Ann.

"Mine too," said Olive.

After they had said their prayers, imploring God to have mercy on them, they drifted in and out of a short, troubled sleep haunted by wild, frantic dreams.

They awoke after a few hours and were surprised to see two bark skirts lying beside their resting place. These were made from the soft inner bark of the cottonwood tree which grew in abundance along the riverbanks. They put them on and discarded the tattered rags they had been wearing for the past year since their capture by the Apaches. Olive was self-conscious at first. She had been brought up to be modest, and baring her breasts in public was unthinkable.

"If our parents could only see us now. They would be shocked," said Mary Ann.

"What choice do we have, Mary Ann? There's nothing left of our dresses. It's better that we look exactly like them than to stand out by wearing our filthy rags."

Olive and Mary Ann were conscious of being watched constantly. This created an atmosphere of mistrust and apprehension as the captives questioned the motives of these Mojaves. Mary Ann asked, "What do they intend to do with us, Olive?"

To which Olive replied, "I wish I knew, Mary Ann. Surely they did not purchase us for purely humanitarian reasons. No, I think we shall know soon enough how they intend to use us."

On the positive side, the location and scenery of their new home were much more pleasant than the Apache village with its dry, desolate surroundings.

The valley extended about thirty or forty miles, northeast by southwest, and varied from two to five miles in width. Through its entire length flowed the beautiful Colorado River, in places a rapid, rushing stream, in others quiet and noiseless where it ran deep. In the spring, when the mountain snows melted, it came roaring and thundering along its rockbound banks, threatening the whole valley and doing some damage. It was a season of great rejoicing when the Colorado overflowed its banks, as they depended on these overflows to irrigate the soil and prepare it for an autumn harvest.

In autumn, they planted the wheat carefully in hills with their fingers, and in the spring, they planted melons, corn, and a few garden vegetables. They knew very little about agriculture. When Olive and Mary Ann arrived among them, the wheat sown the previous fall had germinated and looked green and healthy, but it did not appear nearly enough to maintain one-fifth of their population.

"Look, Mary Ann," said Olive. "They spend more time raising twenty spears of wheat from one hill than it would have taken to cultivate an acre with the methods we use."

However, seeing those scattered parcels of green reminded Olive and Mary Ann of the home they had left behind.

Chapter XVIII
Cairook

For a time, after their coming among the Mojaves, little was said to the captives. Topeka told them they were to remain in the chief's house, but they were regarded as strange intruders for whom their owners had no sympathy. Olive interpreted their attitude to mean, "you may live here if you will bow, uncomplaining, to our barbarism and privations."

After a few days, the Mojaves began to order the captives to bring wood and water and to perform errands. Olive and Mary Ann soon learned that their condition was that of unmitigated slavery, not just to the adults, but to the children as well. In this respect, it was similar to their life among the Apaches. In a narrative version of Olive's captivity, written by Royal B. Stratton, Olive is quoted as saying,

Their whimpering, idiotic children very soon learned to dictate orders to us with all the authority of kings and queens. These slovenly creatures would find chores for us, simply to gratify their love of command. Any hurried attention to them was grounds for punishment, either of whipping or withholding of food. The adults of the tribe seemed to enjoy seeing the white captives subjugated by their children.

The Colorado had overflowed during the winter, and there had been ample rain. The Mojaves were in high hopes of a bountiful crop during this season. What was, to them, a rich harvest would be considered a poor yield by the whites. If the least skilled white farmer had access to this Mojave valley, it would have been as productive and fruitful as any seen in white man's territory. However, the Mojaves were indolent and lazy, and what little effort they put into tilling the land was wasted due to inferior methods. While they had the superior natural advantage of rich soil and a source of irrigation, they lacked ambition in the area of agriculture and preferred the excitement of war.

Nothing occurred during the summer of 1852 to offer hope of escape to the captive girls. It was not long before they were able to understand the Mojaves in conversation. Every day, they heard expressions of hate directed toward the white race. The women would question Olive and Mary Ann closely, attempting to draw from them any discontent they might feel in their servile condition. They taunted the captives in a less ferocious manner than the Apaches, but with obvious hate of the "good-for-nothing whites."

A few Mojaves wanted to learn the language of the whites. Among these was Cairook, a young man of some conceit and arrogance. One day, he approached Olive.

"How do you like living with the Mojaves?"

"I do not like it as well as among the whites, for we do not have enough to eat," she replied.

"We have enough to satisfy us. You *Americanos* work hard, and it does you no good. We enjoy ourselves."

"We enjoy ourselves well at home, and all our people seem happier than any Indian I have seen."

"Our great fathers worked just as you whites do, and they had many nice things to wear, but the flood came and swept the old folks away. A white son of the family stole all the arts and clothing, and the Mojaves have had none since."

"But if our people had this beautiful valley, they would till it and raise much grain. You Mojaves don't like to work, and you say you don't have enough to eat, but it is because you are lazy."

At this, he became furious. His black eyes threatened to leap from their sockets, and his fists clenched ominously. For a moment, she thought he might strike her, but he turned and left in helpless rage.

As soon as he had gone, Olive was sorry for her harsh words, for, although she believed them to be true, they had deeply wounded Cairook, who had never been unkind to her or Mary Ann.

Olive frequently told the Mojaves how grain, cattle, and fowl would abound if this fertile land were in control of the whites. This never failed to elicit their wrath and taunts, but sometimes they were curious.

One day, several of them were questioning Olive about her former home, the white nation, and the ways in which the whites made their living. Olive told them about tilling the soil and, using a stick, drew a picture of a plow in the sand. She drew oxen and hitched them to her plow. She told them how the plow would break the soil. For a while, they were curious and attentive, but then they spewed forth a volley of scorn and derision toward Olive and the white race in general.

Olive told them of the abundance that rewarded white labor, while the Indians had so little. They said, "Your ancestors were dishonest, and their children are weak. By and by, the pride and good living of the whites will ruin them. You have forsaken nature and want to possess the earth, but you will not be able to."

In conversing with them, Olive learned of a superstition held by the Mojaves regarding the distinction between the red and the white races. They said, pointing to a high mountain at the northern end of the valley, "In ancient time, there was a flood that covered the entire world, except that mountain, and all the present races were merged in one family, and this family was saved from the deluge by climbing up to that mountaintop. This ancient family was very large and had great riches: clothing, cattle, horses, and plenty to eat. When the water subsided, one of the family took all of the cattle and clothing and headed north. They were turned from red to white and remained in the north. Another part of this family took deer skins and bark, and from these, the Indians came. All of the ancient family were red, until the progenitor of the whites stole; then he was turned white. The *Hiccos* (dishonest whites) will lose their cattle yet. This thieving will be their downfall."

They told Olive that remains of the old "big house" in which this ancient family had lived were still up there, as well as shards of jugs, broken pots, and remnants of all the various articles used by them. They believed that, ever since the great flood, this mountain had been the abode of spirits and that these spirits were aware of all the doings of the tribe, even the secret motives and character of each individual.

Furthermore, this mountain was consecrated to these spirits, and if the feet of mortals should presume to tread upon this spirit land, a fire would burst from the mountain and instantly consume them, except those who were selected and appointed by these spirits to communicate special messages to the tribe.

These chosen ones were generally the medicine men, and when a war was indicated by these master spirits, they signaled their intentions by causing the mountain to shoot forth great tongues of fire, visible only to the medicine men. The time, place, object, and method of the war were communicated to the medicine men and then to the chief. However, the power of the chief was absolute, and if he ordained to alter the terms of war dictated by the spirits, the medicine men would have a "second consultation" with the spirits to modify the time or method of warfare to coincide with the wishes of the chief.

Another legend held that in the region of this sacred mountain, the spirits of every *Hicco* that the Mojaves had slain were held in chains and that their souls were eternally doomed to a torment of fierce, quenchless fires, and that any Mojave who had slain a *Hicco* would be exalted to eternal honors and privileges thereafter.

Olive and Mary Ann were cautioned not to attempt the rescue of these *"Hicco* spirits," or they would share in a like fate.

During these questioning sessions, Olive noticed that Cairook stood, listening, on the perimeter of the group. He was easily distinguished by his superior height, being much taller than the average Mojave. When the others had left, he would approach Olive and speak to her in English. He was eager to learn more of the language, and if she had a few moments of free time, she would teach him. He was intelligent and learned quickly. He told her he was twenty-one years old and that he lived in the men's lodge.

These English classes were brief, due to Olive's heavy schedule of chores. Invariably, they were interrupted by one of the squaws ordering her to fetch firewood or roots, or to perform some other menial task. Olive soon found herself looking forward to Cairook's visits.

One day, she asked Topeka if she knew Cairook. Topeka laughed.

"Yes, I know him. He is my brother."

"Your brother? But why does he not live with you?"

"When a boy becomes a man, he no longer lives with his parents. He must live in the men's lodge and learn our laws and how to be a warrior. He is instructed by those who have experienced battle and who know how to make and use weapons of war. They learn how to outwit the enemy and kill them."

Olive felt a shudder run through her body as she recalled the murder of her family. Was Cairook capable of such barbarity? She put it out of her mind. She didn't want to know.

Topeka went on to tell her that Cairook would be chief when her father died. Olive couldn't help thinking that he would make a fine chief someday.

One day, Cairook approached Olive as she worked in her little garden beside the chief's house.

"I have made a plow," he said proudly. He produced a V-shaped piece of metal from behind his back.

"Where did you get that?" she asked.

"A Yuma brought the rim of a wagon wheel for me to play with when I was a boy. He said he had found it near the fort. I rolled it around the village 'til I tired of it and left it behind my father's house. When you drew the plow in the sand, I thought of the old rim. I found it where I had left it and cut it to make the plow."

"It's very good, Cairook," she said.

"You may keep it. Someday, all my people will have plows with strong horses to pull them. Then we will plant many seeds and have fine crops."

"I'm sure you will, Cairook," she said, realizing that she meant it.

Chapter XIX
The Tattoo

There was little game in the Mojave Valley, and very little meat was consumed by the tribe. On the rare occasions that meat became available, only men were allowed to eat it. At some seasons, they were able to procure fish from a small lake in the vicinity, but the lake would dry up in summer, becoming little more than a mud hole. As for grain and vegetables, they hardly produced enough for four months, when, with proper agricultural practices, they could have produced for a year. It pained Olive to see these "live-for-the-day savages" pick and eat vegetables before they were fully grown.

Olive and Mary Ann spent most of the summer in hard work. They were roused at daybreak, baskets were swung from their shoulders, and they were obliged to walk six to eight miles for the mesquite seed which grew on a bush the size of a manzanita. In the first part of the season, the mesquite bush bloomed with a small yellow flower. After a few weeks, a large seed pod could be gathered from it. This was the principal staple food of the Mojave tribe. They hung these seeds up in their huts to be dried and ate them when their grain and vegetable supply was exhausted. The captives spent from dawn to dusk gathering these pods, and often, they could not fill their basket in a day due to the scarcity that first year. For their failure, they were severely chastised. Olive was later quoted as saying,

I could endure my daily tasks, but to see the demands made upon little Mary Ann, day after day, by these unfeeling wretches, as many of them were, when her constitution was already broken down and she was suffering the most excruciating pain, was more severe punishment than any I had to endure. I often thought it would be a sad relief to see poor Mary Ann sink into the grave beyond the oppression and the cruel treatment she was subjected to. But there were times, after a rest that her captors were obliged to grant due to her utter incapacity, that she would appear refreshed.

Several times during that first year, their captors would accuse Olive and Mary Ann of plotting their escape. They would frequently question them about their feelings toward their captivity. Though the girls persisted in denying any plans to escape, many did not believe them. They warned the girls against such an undertaking, assuring them that the Mojaves would follow them to the white settlements, if necessary, and upon their recapture, they would be tortured in the most painful manner.

One day, when Olive and Mary Ann returned from digging roots, they entered the chief's hut to turn over the contents of their baskets. Two medicine men and some of their followers came to the door of the hut. Aespaneo, the chief's wife, spoke to the girls.

"Go out into the yard. The medicine men are going to put marks on your faces."

Olive and Mary Ann did not understand at first, but Aespaneo made it clear by her motions that they were going to have their faces tattooed. They had seen these tattoos on other females of the tribe, and they had hoped to be spared this painful, disfiguring experience.

"Oh, please, I beg of you, don't put marks on our faces," cried Olive.

But it was all in vain. They said,

"We know why you object. It is because you expect to return to the whites, and you would be ashamed of it then, but you will never return. You belong to the Mojaves, and you will wear our *ki-e-chook.* If you should get away, or if some other tribe should steal you, we will know you by these marks."

The medicine men pricked the skin on the girls' chins in small, regular rows with a very sharp stick until they bled freely. Then they dipped these sticks in the juice of a certain weed that grew on the banks of the river, and then in the powder of a blue stone that was found in low water in the stream bed. This stone was first burned so that it would pulverize easily, and this burning turned the powder nearly black. Then they worked this fine powder into the lacerated parts of the face.

This process was somewhat painful, and for two or three days following the procedure, it pained even more. They were told these marks could never be eradicated from their faces. With this crushing blow, Olive and Mary Ann saw whatever dim hope they may have had fade into despair and hopelessness. At night, they lay awake crying.

"Look at us, Olive. We are marked for life. Even if we should escape and find our way back to the whites, they will know we have been marked by the Indians, and they will have nothing to do with us. We are ugly now. How could God let this happen?"

"Mary Ann, I wish I knew. But, as bad as our situation is right now, surely God has not forsaken us completely. We may think ourselves ugly, but God still loves us, and we must believe in Him, because without our faith, we have nothing."

"Of course, you're right, Olive. Thank God we have each other. Without you, I would have no reason to live."

Olive hugged her little sister close, their tears intermingling, until they finally fell into an exhausted sleep.

Chapter XX
Famine

Autumn was, by far, the easiest season of the year, but it was one of continuous drudgery. There was very little rain that winter, and the Colorado did not overflow its banks. Towards spring, their grain was exhausted. The grain that had been newly planted came up much later than usual and looked sickly once it had germinated. It held little promise for the next year, and the Mojaves were uneasy. There were no provisions or food of any kind to eat in the village that would sustain its population of over fifteen hundred for two days

Olive and Mary Ann were driven forth at daybreak every morning, in cold, rough winds, to glean any old, dry mesquite seed that might have escaped their exhausting search during the summer and autumn months. From this time until the gathering of the meager harvest of that year, they were barely able to survive. In return for their strenuous labor, they were given a little dry corn in small quantities. Their apprehension grew as they anticipated worse privation awaiting them the next year. No rain had fallen during the spring to do much good. This harvest was next to nothing.

After holding back the seed grain for the next crop, there wasn't a month's supply left over. They had gathered very little mesquite during the summer, and nothing short of starvation could be expected. This knowledge threw a cloak of despair upon Olive and Mary Ann and blotted out any remote hope of survival. They were aware that, when deprivation occurred, their portion would be meted out after the tribe had supplied themselves. They had seen these Mojaves become more savage and implacable in times of adversity. Olive was more worried about Mary Ann than herself. Mary Ann had never been strong. Olive recalled that her mother had always worried about Mary Ann's frailty, though she had begun reading at four and insisted on attending school every day. Olive was afraid Mary Ann could not stand the rigors of deprivation. She would often say, "Oh, Olive, if only I could have one dish of bread and milk. I would enjoy it so much."

The Mojave would grind mesquite seed between stones and make a mush by adding water. Olive and Mary Ann disliked mesquite mush. They considered it tasteless and nauseating. However, as the supply of this staple diminished, they were put on a stinted allowance of it, as it was the only food available.

During the first autumn, Aespaneo gave them some seed grain, corn, and melon seeds. She showed them about thirty feet square of ground marked off where they could plant and raise it for themselves. Olive and Mary Ann were thrilled and thanked Aespaneo profusely. They eagerly planted the wheat and carefully concealed the handful of corn and melon seeds to plant in the spring. They enjoyed these hours of working the soil, as it reminded them of happier days on their family farm in Illinois.

"Olive, do you remember how lovely the wheat fields were when the wind would come up and ripple through them? I would give anything to be back there now."

"Perhaps we will see it again. Miracles do happen, Mary Ann. We must try to stay positive and think happy thoughts, no matter how bad things get."

To keep their spirits up, they would sing the hymns they learned in church as they worked in their little garden. One day, Aespaneo heard them singing and invited them to entertain the chief's visitors. The visitors, mostly sub-chiefs and their wives, were delighted with their singing. They rewarded Olive and Mary Ann with beads and bits of red cloth, which were highly prized among the Mojave. Topeka begged them to teach her how to sing these hymns.

"Please teach me to sing as you do. I would like to sing with you."

The girls did their best to teach Topeka a few hymns, and, though she had trouble with the English words, she had a lovely, clear voice and soon learned to carry a tune. Prior to this, she had done some chanting in the Indian style, but never anything like this.

"If you can't master the words, Topeka, just hum along or make up words. No one will notice as long you sing along with us," Mary Ann encouraged.

Topeka smiled and patted Mary Ann's head.

In the back of Olive's mind was the apprehension that, before they could harvest their crop, famine might lay their bodies in the dust. Winter was fast approaching, and Olive dreaded the frozen nights and lack of food. She saw the effect this deprivation was having on Mary Ann as she became thinner and weaker.

The Indians said that, about sixty miles away, there was a *taneta* (tree) that bore a berry called *oth-te-toa,* upon which they had subsisted for some time several years before. It could only be reached by a rugged and mountainous path of sixty miles. Soon, a large party set out in search of this tree. Many women, accustomed to bearing burdens, were not able to go. Mary Ann started, but soon gave out and had to return. A few men accompanied them, but it was a disgrace for them to bear burdens, this befitting only squaws and captives. Olive was commanded to take her basket and go with them.

On the third day, they reached the place and found the *taneta* to be a bush very much like the mesquite, with a much larger leaf. It grew from five to thirty feet in height. The berry was much more pleasant to the taste than the mesquite. The juice, when extracted and mixed with water, was very similar to the orange. Olive was willing to put up with any hardship in order to prolong Mary Ann's life. She had seemed depressed and quite ill when Olive left her.

After wandering about for two days with little results, six members of the group started in quest of some place where the *oth-te-toa* might be more abundant. They traveled over twenty miles from their temporary camp, but found *tanetas* in abundance and loaded with the berries. They had reached a field never found before. They filled their baskets and hastened to join the camp party before they headed to the village.

They soon lost their way and wandered the entire night without water. They were all sick from eating their *oth-te-toa* berries. Towards day, nearly exhausted, with three of their group very sick, they were forced to halt. They nursed the sick, sweating them with the medicinal leaf always kept with them, but their efforts were in vain. Before noon, the three had breathed their last. A fire was kindled, and their bodies were burned.

For several hours, Olive expected to be laid on one of those funeral pyres in that dark, trackless wilderness. She thought she had suffered more during that two or three hours than any other time in her captivity. They resumed their search for the camp. Some of them took the baskets of the dead and struggled to keep up. The rest of the party went howling through the woods, mourning the dead.

The next day, they found the camp and were soon on their way. They traveled all night and arrived at the village. Olive went immediately to see Mary Ann and found that she was much worse. She had been furnished with scarcely enough food to keep her alive. Olive did everything she could to help her, and for a short time, she revived. The *oth-te-toa* berry, while it would add to their flesh and give them an appearance of health (if their stomachs could take it), had but little nutritional value.

Olive searched, sometimes entire days, for blackbird eggs for Mary Ann. These eggs were plentiful in season, but not at that time of year. When Olive was fortunate enough to find a few, they were very much relished by Mary Ann. For a while, Olive hoped that, with care and nursing, Mary Ann might survive until spring, when fish might become available.

The berries that had been gathered were soon consumed by the tribe, and it was extremely difficult for Olive to find a morsel of food. The ground was searched for miles, and every root was gathered. Olive walked great distances in search of a place where roots might still be found. Sometimes, she was so hungry she would pull the root from the ground and eat it quickly before it could be snatched away from her. Sometimes, she was fortunate in finding the root of a reed that grew in the backwaters of the river. These were quite good.

She became adept at throwing rocks and could accurately hit a bird or a rat. When she was fortunate enough to find and kill one of these treasures, she would quickly hide it in her basket and take it back to cook for dinner. She would eat the flesh and feed the broth to Mary Ann, who had become too weak to digest food.

The Indians became reckless and quarrelsome as they selfishly struggled for their own lives without regard for their fellow tribesmen. Every night, there was the smell of burning flesh in the air as the dead were cremated. She was afraid that, if Mary Ann should die, the medicine men would come for her body and burn it. She noticed that the medicine men and their associates that came to remove the dead looked well-nourished compared to the rest of the tribe, who were skin and bones by now. She suspected that those who came to fetch the bodies for cremation were actually eating them.

Chapter XXI
Death of Mary Ann

Mary Ann failed quickly. She and Olive were sometimes without food for whole days at a time. Once in a while, Topeka would give them a morsel to satisfy their cravings. Often, Mary Ann would say, "I am well enough, but I want something to eat—then I should be well."

Olive could not leave her overnight. There were no roots, but even if Olive could travel a distance and find some, their lazy captors would take them for their own children. Several children had died, and more were dying. Each death that occurred was the occasion of loud howling.

Mary Ann was weak and growing weaker, and Olive gave up in despair. She sat by Mary Ann's side for a few days, begging the passing Indians to give her something to keep Mary Ann alive. Sometimes, she succeeded. Had it not been for the wife and daughter of the chief, they would have obtained nothing. They seemed to really feel for the captives and would have done more if it had been in their power.

Mary Ann would speak of "dear Pa and Ma" and say, "They suffered an awful death, but they are now safe and happy in a better and brighter land, while I am left to starve among savages."

She now regarded life as no longer worth preserving, and she expressed wishes of longing to die. One day, she called Olive to her side and said, "Olive, I shall die soon, but you will live to get away. I shall soon be with Father and Mother and my dear brothers and sisters."

Then she asked Olive to sing the evening hymn they had been taught by their parents. She joined her sweet, clear voice with Olive's, and together they sang, "The day is past and gone. The evening shades appear ..."

The tears ran freely down Olive's face.

"Don't cry, Olive. I go to a better place. Sing the hymn, 'How Tedious and Tasteless the Hour When Jesus I No Longer See.'"

Olive tried to sing, but could not get beyond the first line. Mary Ann sang the entire hymn, then gradually sank away.

During her singing, quite a crowd had gathered and seemed much surprised. Some of them stood and gazed upon her for almost an hour while their own kindred were dying in other parts of the village. Among them were Topeka and her mother, the wife of the chief, Aespaneo.

That day, Aespaneo approached and listened to Mary Ann sing. For some time, she bent over Mary Ann, looked into her face, touched her face, and suddenly broke out in the most pitiful wailing. She wept from the heart. If she were Mary Ann's mother, she could not have shown more emotion. She sobbed, she moaned, she howled. She sat there, next to Mary Ann, all night.

The next morning, Mary Ann called Olive to her side and said, "I am willing to die. I shall be much better off there."

Then her strength failed. She tried to sing, but was too weak. A number of the tribe, men, women, and children, surrounded her. Aespaneo watched her every moment. Mary Ann died a few minutes later. Among the tribe's revived records, though unwritten, there is an account of the death of the American captive in the doorway of the chief's *pasiado.* It made a lasting impression on those who had witnessed her peaceful passing.

When Olive saw that Mary Ann was dead, she felt a great loneliness and despair. She wished that she could lie down in the icy embrace that stiffened the delicate limbs of her beloved sister. She felt that she would die soon by the slow torture of starvation and thought about ending her life at once. She considered stealing a morsel of food and attempting an escape.

Aespaneo and Topeka manifested a sympathy that Olive had not seen since she had lived among the whites. Now, at the direction of the chief, preparations had begun to burn Mary Ann's body, in the Mojave tradition. This Olive could not endure. She found a quiet place and prayed. Her dark, suicidal thoughts disappeared, and she resigned herself to her lot. She returned to look upon the peaceful countenance of her sister one last time.

Standing by the corpse, she looked up to see Aespaneo approaching. She told Olive that she had interceded with the chief and that he had finally agreed that Olive could dispose of Mary Ann's body as she saw fit. Olive wept tears of gratitude and thanked her. The chief gave Olive two blankets, and with the assistance of Aespaneo and Topeka, she wrapped the corpse. Orders were then given to two Indians to follow Olive's directions in disposing of Mary Ann's body.

Olive selected a spot in the little garden plot the two girls had planted. They dug a grave about five feet deep, and into it they gently lowered Mary Ann's remains. As sand was pushed into the grave, covering her little sister's frail body, the painful past rushed across Olive's mind. Now the last of her family was gone.

It was the first and only grave in that valley. Olive looked around her at the large company of half-dressed savages, some serious, some mourning, and some laughing at this novel method of disposing of the dead. Others watched in breathless silence, thinking, no doubt, *This is what white folks do.* Olive longed to plant a rose on her grave, but this was denied her. Flowers did not exist for the Mojaves.

After the burial, Olive seemed to lose her energy. She felt faint and weak. She got little strength from the scant rations dealt to her. She became more and more disposed to close her eyes and sink into an untroubled sleep. This was the only time she really longed to die and end her suffering. But Aespaneo, the wife of the chief, again came to her in the depths of her despair with some corn gruel in a hollow stone. Olive wondered how she had obtained it.

"Aespaneo, where did you get this?" she asked.

"I had hidden some corn for spring planting. I took part of it, ground it to a coarse meal, and added water."

Olive took this gruel gratefully, and soon Aespaneo brought her more.

Olive began to revive. She felt a new life and strength, not just from the gruel, but from the genuine outpouring of sympathy from this Indian woman. Aespaneo had the discretion to deny the cravings that had been kindled by the small quantity she brought at first and dispensed a little at a time until, within three days, Olive regained a cheerfulness and vigor she had not had in weeks. Aespaneo did this in a surreptitious way, cautioning Olive not to speak of it. She had done it when some of her own family were starving. The woman had buried that corn to keep it from the lazy crowd around her who would have devoured it in a moment. She did it when death and sickness were occurring every day in the village. If not for her, Olive would have perished.

By her own efforts, Olive was able to procure a little to nourish her half-starved stomach. By using half of the seed corn she and Mary Ann had hidden and supplementing this with a small amount of bitter, fermented *oth-te-toa* soup, she was able to survive.

Chapter XXII
War with the Cocopah

The Colorado overflowed during the early spring of 1854, guaranteeing a good harvest for the tribe in the coming autumn. Olive took pains to guard the little wheat garden that she and Mary Ann had planted the autumn before. She also planted a few kernels of corn and some melon seeds. Day after day, she watched her little garden to protect it from birds. She knew she could not survive another winter like the last.

Aespaneo watched Olive's garden when she was out gathering roots. She nearly lost her corn to the blackbirds as they descended from the skies and attacked her garden mercilessly. They were not the only predators. There were some who had a horror of honest labor who watched her little corn patch with hungry and thieving eyes and, if not for the chief and Aespaneo, would have eaten the corn green while still in the ear. As reward for Olive's hard work and vigilant watching, she would reap about one-half bushel of corn and about the same quantity of wheat at harvest time in autumn. The melons she had planted did not survive.

During the spring, while her crops were beginning to grow, she subsisted principally upon fish from the lake and a small root about the size of a hazelnut which she procured by traveling long distances. Sometimes, after a long, exhausting search, she would return with a handful of these roots and was forced to share them with some stout, lazy Indians who had been sunning themselves all day by the river.

Olive felt cheerful again, except those times when she thought of Mary Ann. Then loneliness and desolation would overcome her and depress her spirit. Aespaneo, the same woman who had saved her life, furnished her with a small plot and seed to raise corn and wheat, and watched it for her for many days, now interceded with the chief to secure a place where Olive could store her produce when it was ready to be harvested in autumn. She also secured a promise from Espaniole that only Olive should have access to it.

Cairook, who had begun to visit Olive more frequently, confided to her in the early spring of 1854 that the council had begun to lay plans for a war upon the Cocopahs, a tribe several hundred miles away. He said, "I will be one of sixty warriors who will fight and conquer the Cocopahs, the enemy of the Mojave."

"What is to be gained from this war with the Cocopahs?" she asked.

He was somewhat taken aback by this question. Then he spoke with conviction.

"An ancient prophecy tells us that the Mojaves will conquer the Cocopahs and subject them to our will. There have been other battles, and the Mojaves have always triumphed. The Mojave will succeed in vanquishing their enemies. It has been ordained by the spirits."

Bows, arrows, war clubs, and stone knives were prepared in abundance. The war clubs were made of a very solid wood that came from the tree called *cooachee,* which grew on the mountain. It was very hard and heavy. Olive had never seen such industry among the male tribesmen. They seemed driven by a purpose.

Preparations were also made by the squaws, although most of them were opposed to the expedition. Those who had husbands, sons, and brothers tried everything in their power to dissuade them from fighting. The squaws accused them of foolishness and a lust for war and begged them not to risk their lives and those of their dependents.

It had been rumored that, since the last attack on them, the Cocopahs had formed alliances with several surrounding tribes who would come to their aid if attacked. The women argued that the newly strengthened Cocopahs would be able to avenge past injury and conquer the Mojaves. Their pleas went unheeded, and, on the day of departure, the whole tribe turned out to bid their warriors farewell and good fortune. It was a time of wild, savage excitement and deep mourning.

Olive soon learned that, so far as her life was concerned, she had an interest in the success of this expedition. Shortly after the warriors had left the village, a tribal elder came to see her. After exchanging perfunctory greetings, he said, "It is the custom of the Mojaves that if any of our warriors should be slain in battle, the lives of prisoners or captives must be sacrificed, in like number, by the most terrible torture. This is not done to appease our gods, as we have none. It is done as a gift to the spirits of those men who have sacrificed their lives for the good of our tribe. Your life must pay for the death of the first Mojave killed by the enemy."

This information was delivered dispassionately with no apologies. Olive was terrified. She could not believe that she had barely survived starvation only to die in this most hideous manner.

·

·

Chapter XXIII
Mojaves Triumph

Olive had recently learned that she was not much further from the white settlements than when she was among the Apaches. Parties of Mojave occasionally made excursions to the settlements, and there was talk of increasing trade with the Mexicans and whites. Olive began to hope that she might somehow make her situation known and be rescued from captivity. Now, she was faced with the choice between making an immediate effort to escape, which would cost her life if caught, or wait in dreadful suspense in hopes that no Mojave warrior would be slain Just as things had appeared brighter, she was thrown into gloomy apprehensions for her life

For the next forty-five days, Olive lay awake at night contemplating her fate. The faint hope that she had felt when she learned of the tribe's plans to increase trade with the Mexicans and whites evaporated with the realization that she might not live that long.

One warm, sunny day in mid-April, Olive was out gathering roots and, returning a little before sunset, she saw an Indian approaching at some distance beyond the village. He was descending a hill to the river from the other side, but she could not tell if he was a Yuma or a Mojave. These two tribes were on friendly terms, and frequent news-carriers passed between them. Olive watched closely as he half-ran and half-stumbled down the embankment, obviously exhausted. He descended into the river, and as he emerged again upon the near bank, she recognized him. He was Ohitia, a Mojave warrior, but why was he returning alone? Fear gripped her heart. Was he the lone survivor of the battle? She knew that, for her, the decisive hour had come.

Her approach to the village had not been observed. She stood, frozen with fear. She considered heading back the way she had come and attempting her escape at nightfall. She looked around her.

Mountains loomed on every side. If there were trails through those mountains, she was not aware of them.

She saw Ohitia enter a hut on the outskirts of the village. In a few moments, shouting was heard. It spread throughout the village, and people began to run toward the river and the foothills beyond. Olive couldn't hear what they were shouting, but she began to walk toward the chief's hut to await her fate. She imagined she saw her doom written in the faces of every Mojave she met along the way. No one spoke to her.

As she sat silently in the empty chief's hut, a crowd began to gather outside. In the approaching darkness, a fire was lit, and Ohitia stood up to speak. Olive watched, her heart pounding in her ears. She held her breath and felt as if she were going to faint.

Ohitia spoke: "Mojaves have triumphed—five prisoners taken—all on their way—none of our warriors killed—they will be here tomorrow."

Olive's breath suddenly escaped in a gasp. She nearly collapsed in relief. Tears of gratitude ran down her face. She silently thanked God for sparing her life and saving her from death by torture.

The next day, the women milled about the village, anxiously awaiting the return of their loved ones. They scanned the hillside for any sign of the approaching warriors. At the sight of the first handful of braves as they came over the crest of the hill, several women leaped into the river in unbridled joy. Soon, the braves joined them as more continued to descend the bank and enter the river.

Soon, the river was alive with men and women, whooping, splashing, and hugging. They emerged from the river, laughing and dripping wet, as they slowly headed to their hogans.

Olive stood on the shore, her eyes fixed on the hillside on the opposite bank. Then she saw Topeka watching and waiting too. She walked over to Topeka.

"Have you seen Cairook?" she asked timidly.

Topeka turned to look at her, a puzzled look on her face. Then she smiled.

"Why, Olive, do you love my brother?"

Olive felt the color rising in her face.

"Of course not. It is my wish for you and your family that your brother returns unharmed."

Topeka gave her a skeptical look and turned back to the river, where several more braves were now crossing.

"Oh, look, there he is," she shouted.

Together, they raced toward the riverbank, where Cairook was emerging from the river. The water glistened on his tall, naked body, and the wet loincloth clung to him, revealing the outline of his manhood. He was the conquering hero, awesome and every inch a chief. Olive felt her knees buckle at the sight of him, and she was afraid she might fall.

Topeka hugged her brother while Olive stood shyly to the side. Then Cairook turned and looked directly at her, riveting her to the spot with his dark, penetrating eyes. She felt the color rise in her cheeks and averted her eyes.

That night, in her blankets, she scolded herself.

"You must not think about Cairook. You are a slave, and he will be great chief someday. Furthermore, he is a savage. If your father were still alive, he would be furious."

But try as she would, she could not erase the glorious image of Cairook emerging from the river, shining like the Adonis she had seen in one of her old schoolbooks.

The next day, four more men came in with the captives, and within a few days, all had returned. There were no serious injuries. The day after the coming of the last stragglers, a meeting of the whole tribe was called. There was great rejoicing which lasted several days. They danced, sang, shouted, and played their cornstalk flutes until all were exhausted. It was their custom never to eat salted meat until the next moon after the coming of a captive among them. Therefore, they did not eat salt fish for several days.

CRUCIFIXION OF NOWEREHA

Chapter XXIV
Crucifixion of Nowereha

Among the captives they had stolen from the Cocopahs was a fair- complexioned young woman of about twenty-five years. She was the most beautiful Indian woman Olive had ever seen. She was tall, graceful, and lady-like in her appearance. Her skin was lighter than the Mojaves or the other Cocopah captives. While the other captives appeared well and indifferent to their plight, the woman's face and eyes betrayed an awful grief.

The woman was named Nowereha. Her language was as foreign to the Mojaves as English. The other captives were girls from twelve to sixteen years old, and while they displayed a "don't-care" attitude, Nowereha was overcome with grief. She ate but little food and kept up a constant moaning and wailing, except when threatened by her captors. Olive was very curious about her and tried to learn the circumstances under which she had been torn from her home. She attempted to converse with Nowereha.

With much difficulty, Olive learned what had happened, and it fully explained her extreme sadness. Their village had been attacked in the night by Mojave warriors, and, after a short battle, the Cocopahs had taken flight. The Mojaves pursued them. Nowereha had a child about two months old, but, after running a short distance, her husband had caught up with her, taken the baby, and run on ahead. She was overtaken and captured by the Mojaves.

For one week, Nowereha wandered about the village by day, the perfect image of desperation and despair. At times, she appeared to be insane. She slept very little. The cruel Mojaves who had taken her knew well the cause of her grief. They knew that they had robbed her of her child, and they watched her closely. They showed no interest or concern for her, except to mock or torment her.

One morning, there was whispering throughout the village that Nowereha was missing. Olive remembered seeing Topeka giving Nowereha some corn, and, after grinding some of it, Nowereha had made a cake of it and hidden it in her dress. There was a prolonged search of the village and the huts to which the other captives had been assigned. This took some time, for which Olive was grateful, as she was hopeful that Nowereha would have a head start on her escape.

When they realized that she was attempting to return to her village, a search party was sent out. A day and night passed, and Olive began to hope for the safety of the fugitive. Some of the Indians believed she might have drowned herself in the river.

Several days after this, just before nightfall, a Yuma Indian suddenly came into camp, driving a woman before him. With a sinking heart, Olive realized it was Nowereha. Her hair was disheveled, her old woolen clothes torn, her eyes swollen, and every feature of her noble face distorted.

Runners were kept constantly on the trail between the Mojaves and the Yumas, bearing news from tribe to tribe. These runners would have certain stations where they would meet to exchange news. Then each would return to his own tribe with the news. At times, when the news was urgent, great signal fires would be built, and messages would be telegraphed by smoke signals which were understood by both tribes.

About four days after Nowereha's escape, one of these Yuma runners was approaching a meeting station on the trail between the two tribes when he noticed a woman under a shelf of rock on the opposite bank of the river. He immediately suspected that this was the captive the Mojaves were searching for. He plunged into the stream and seized her. She struggled, but he subdued her by force. He immediately started toward the Mojave village, driving Nowereha before him. It was an unwritten law among the tribes that all escaped captives of a friendly tribe must be returned to that tribe immediately.

Nowereha had traveled one hundred and thirty miles by swimming the river where it was not too rapid or shallow and running alongside when it was impossible to swim. She had only traveled at night until she found a cave under a rock ledge, where she decided to hide until nightfall. That was where the Yuma had found her.

On her return, there were shouts and victory dances. The Mojaves danced around her, screamed in her ears, spat in her face, and made threatening gestures toward her. They made it clear that Nowereha would never have an opportunity to run away again.

The next morning, a post was planted firmly in the ground, and, about eight feet from the ground, a cross-beam was attached to the post. They then drove large, rough, wooden spikes through the palms of Nowereha's hands, and, by these, they lifted her onto the cross and drove the nails into the soft wood of the cross-beam, stretching her arms as far as they could. With pieces of bark impregnated with thorns, they tied her head firmly back to the upright post, drove spikes through her ankles, and left her in this condition.

They rounded up the other Cocopah captives, and, placing Olive with them, ordered them to watch poor Nowereha until she died This was to be a warning to the captives of what would befall them should they attempt to escape. They then commenced to dance around Nowereha in circles, chanting, stamping, and taunting in the most wild and frenzied manner. Olive felt as if she were standing in the very bowels of hell. After this, several of them took up bows and arrows, which they proceeded to fire into Nowereha's quivering flesh. Occasionally, she would cry aloud in the most pitiful manner. This would elicit deafening yells from the heartless mob.

She hung in this horrible condition for over two hours, all the while bleeding and sighing, her body mangled in the most hideous manner. When they were sure she was dead and they could no longer inflict pain on her, they took her body down, hauled it to a funeral pyre, and burned it. Olive felt faint but would not give these fiends the satisfaction of seeing her sink to the ground. Instead, she walked proudly toward the chief's hut, and, slipping quickly behind it, she vomited into the soft sand.

Chapter XXV
The "Wedding"

She had come to know the direction in which the whites lived by watching the route the Mojaves took on their occasional visits to the white settlements. She had thought of traveling in that direction when she made her escape, but the memory of Nowereha's horrible fate deterred her. She had not entirely given up hope, but was now determined to make the best of her circumstances and take whatever joy she could each day.

She waited until she had gained sufficient control of her emotions. Then, she entered the chief's hut. There was a small fire burning, and by its light, she was surprised to see the chief, his wife Aespaneo, his daughter Topeka, and his son Cairook. They had not taken part in the torture and killing of Nowereha. Now, they stared at Olive, making her uneasy. After a few moments, the chief spoke: "Olivia, sit here, my child." He gestured toward a space on a blanket between Aespaneo and Topeka.

"You are made sick by what you have seen. I do not condone this, nor can I prevent it. It is Mojave law. If a captive tries to escape, they are killed. It is a warning to other captives that they will suffer a similar fate if they should try to run away. If a Mojave brave is killed in battle, a captive must die to avenge his death. If one of our braves had died in the battle with the Cocopah and no prisoners had been taken, you would have been killed to avenge his death. It could have been you hanging on that cross, Olivia."

He waited until she had had time to ponder this. Then he went on: "We have grown fond of you, and this would bring us great sorrow, but I could do nothing to stop it. I am chief, but I am not above the law.

"Cairook has come here tonight to ask permission to take you as his wife. It is a great honor, as he will be chief when I die. You will no longer need to live in fear of being killed to avenge the death of a brave killed in battle."

He paused and looked at Olive, his dark eyes boring into her very soul.

"What say you?" he demanded.

Olive was stunned and confused. She had never heard of a sub-chief marrying a captive. She turned and looked at Cairook. He spoke: "Olive has told me of the large numbers of whites and of their relentless march to the sea beyond the mountains where the sun sets. The day will come when we will have to bargain with the white man for the survival of our tribe. Olive can teach our children to speak their language and understand their ways so that, when they are grown, they may be able to save the Mojave from being crushed under the heel of the white man's boot." He looked at Olive.

"She will be a good wife and a wise mother," he said.

This was not like any marriage proposal she had read about in the romance novels that Lucy had been so fond of. Cairook had not asked her to marry him, nor had he professed to love her. It seemed more of a proposition than a proposal, but one that was mutually beneficial. Olive would enjoy the relative safety and protection that a wife of a sub-chief was entitled to. For his part, Cairook would have a wife and a teacher for his future offspring, which would give them the advantage of learning to live in the white man's world. She would have liked to hear Cairook say he cared for her, but she was wise enough to keep her counsel. For now, survival was more important than love.

The chief looked at Olive expectantly.

"I will be Cairook's wife." She spoke in a loud, clear voice so that Espaniole could plainly hear her, as old age had diminished his hearing. Later, she would wonder what would have happened if she had refused. One did not say "no" to the chief or his son.

With that settled, Aespaneo and Topeka leapt to their feet. They pulled Olive to her feet and embraced her fondly. Topeka danced around in unbridled joy. The old chief clapped his hands, smiling broadly. For a while, Olive forgot she was among Indians, such was their lavish display of emotion.

Finally, Cairook walked over to her and took her hand. She felt small and safe as she looked up into his kind face. He was the tallest Indian she had ever seen. Looking at him now in the firelight, she suddenly realized that this man would be her husband, and to her surprise, she did not shrink from the prospect. His features were chiseled, with high, prominent cheekbones, unlike the broad, flat faces of most Mojaves. He was also very kind and intelligent. True, he was a savage, but he would be *her* savage, and, strangely, the thought did not repel her.

That night, she could not sleep. She walked to the river and looked up at the stars. She thought about all that had happened, the horrible death of Nowereha, Cairook's proposal, and her reluctant submission. She thought about her father. What would he say if he knew she was about to marry an Indian? She spoke out loud.

"Oh, Papa, I am sorry. Please try to understand; I have no choice." Then she caught herself. "What am I saying? Why am I asking you for permission? Did you ask Mother if she wanted to go into the desert alone? Did you ask any of us? If it hadn't been for your stubborn selfishness and total disregard for the safety of your family, I wouldn't be here." The depth of her anger toward her father shocked her. It was frightening in its intensity, but somehow calming at the same time. She walked back to the chief's hogan. All was quiet. She got into her blanket roll and immediately fell into a deep sleep.

The "marriage" took place a week later in a lovely grove of cottonwoods near the river. It was a warm, sunny day, and the entire tribe came out to witness the ceremony. The old chief officiated. He was flanked by the four medicine men and two sub-chiefs. The old chief called on the spirits, beseeching them to bless this union. When he had concluded the invocation, he turned to Cairook and Olive. He took their hands and placed one of Cairook's hands on top and one below Olive's hands. This signified the dominance of the male partner and his duty to protect his wife. He placed one of his hands on Cairook's shoulder and the other on Olive's shoulder. Looking at Cairook, he said, "You have been and always will be my son."

Looking at Olive, he said, "You are now my daughter."

Then, he said, "I give you both my blessing for a long and happy life with many children."

With these final words, the crowd let out a collective cheer and the festivities began. Food began to appear from everywhere. Corn and mesquite cakes were set out on a long table, while dried fish and jerky were furnished by higher-ranking officials of the tribe. Pots of beans were donated by the more industrious farmers who had hauled water from the river to irrigate their crops when the Colorado failed to overflow. There were gifts of cooking pots, calabashes, utensils, wolf skins, blankets, beads, and squares of red flannel. There was dancing and singing far into the night.

From the little hogan they would occupy while another, more suitable for a sub-chief, was being built, they listened to the festivities until they became aware of each other's bodies. Then slowly, with much tenderness, they consummated their marriage and slept peacefully until dawn.

Chapter XXVI
A Little Family

For the next eighteen months, these Mojaves took more care and exercised more forethought in the matter of their food. They were determined not to suffer through another famine like the one in 1853. Olive was resigned to spending the rest of her life among the Mojave. There were some with whom she had become intimately acquainted and from whom she had received humane and friendly treatment. Some had exhibited genuine kindness. She thought it best to cultivate these friendships and to avoid any occasions which would incur their displeasure. For, although she was now elevated to the position of wife of a sub-chief, she was still a *Hicco,* and there were those who were jealous of her and would make trouble if they could.

There were some for whom she had begun to feel a degree of attachment. Among these were the old chief, Espaniole; his wife, Aespaneo; Topeka; and, of course, Cairook. She still had nightmares about the massacre of her family, but tried to keep negative thoughts at bay

She began to imagine that she was happy, and, at times, she was. About three months after her marriage, Olive became ill. Mornings were particularly distressing. She was nauseous and had difficulty keeping food down.

One morning, while Olive was tending her little garden near the chief's house, Aespaneo came out of the house and greeted her.

"How are you this morning, my daughter?" she asked.

"I have not been well, Mother," she replied.

"What is the problem?" Aespaneo looked worried.

"I have had trouble with my stomach, Mother. I feel as if I were going to vomit all the time."

Aespaneo looked at her intently.

"Have you had your bloody flow?" she asked pointedly.

Olive thought a moment.

"No, Mother, I have not."

"Well, you are with child, then, my dear." Aespaneo could not hide her pleasure.

Olive looked down at her stomach, which appeared to be slightly rounded. She acknowledged that Aespaneo might be right. She was happy and frightened at the same time. A baby, so soon? Was she ready to be a mother? She would have to be. What would Cairook say? He was off on a hunt, but she would tell him as soon as he returned. She now realized that her life was changed forever. She could never go back to civilization now.

That evening, as they were having dinner, Olive told Cairook what his mother had said.

"Is it true?" he asked.

"Yes, I'm sure it is. I have all the signs."

"This is good. When will the child come?"

"I am hoping it will be born in time for Christmas. I would consider it the best gift I have ever received."

"This Christmas, it is the white man's holiday, is it not?"

"Yes, it is a great pow-wow to celebrate the birth of Jesus Christ."

"Do you wish to return to the whites to celebrate Christmas?" he asked suddenly, taking her off guard.

"No, no. Our son will be born here. We will have our own Christmas, just the three of us."

"I am glad. It is not good for you to go to the whites. They will have nothing to do with you because you are the wife of an Indian. Our child would be called 'half-breed,' despised and mistreated."

Olive knew he was right. Here, their child, if it were a male, would be chief someday. Honor versus degradation. The choice was clear. She must remain with the Mojaves.

In late December of 1854, Olive gave birth to a son. She was assisted by a midwife, and her labor was relatively short, considering it was her first child. When it was all over, her baby was wrapped in a small blanket and handed to her. She held him close and marveled at his small, dark perfection. He had a full head of black hair which made him look much older. As she gazed contentedly at this little miracle, he began to make little sucking sounds, and she held him to her breast for his first taste of life.

Cairook was ecstatic. He walked about the village, carrying his newborn and boasting to everyone he saw, "Look at my fine little son. His name is Empote Awatacheech Potachecha. He will be chief some day. Then you can say you saw him on his first day of life."

He held the baby up so that even the smallest child could see him. Olive sat in the door of their fine new hogan, watching him as he strutted about. She was smiling. She felt great tenderness for this man and her tiny son.

Olive took to motherhood as a duck to water. She loved holding Empote-John and playing with him. Cairook had given him his tribal name, Empote Awatacheech Potachecha, but Olive called him John. He was a delightful child, beautiful and alert. When he was almost three months old, Olive became pregnant again. This time, she hoped for a daughter.

DWELLINGS OF THE NATIVES OF THE RIO COLORADO OF THE WEST

MOHAVES PLAYING HOOP GAME
(Cairook's house with Cairook standing on roof)
Painting by Balduin Möllhausen, Whipple Expedition 1854-1855
Round bins were used for food storage
Note woman seated on mound behind house.Could this be Olive?

Chapter XXVII
The Whipple Expedition

In the winter of 1854, the Whipple expedition arrived at the village and were welcomed by the tribe. This was largely due to Lt. Amiel W. Whipple's good judgment, as he brought many gifts, which he presented to the chiefs and which they, in turn, distributed to their people.

Lt. Whipple was commissioned by the U.S. government to survey the thirty-fifth parallel to determine the best route for a new continental railway to be constructed by the Central Pacific Railroad Company.

Accompanying him on this mission were several topographical engineers, interpreters, a German artist named Balduin Müllhausen, and Lt. Joseph C. Ives. Mr. Müllhausen had been commissioned by the Smithsonian Institute to study and sketch the indigenous tribes in the area. Several of his drawings appear in Whipple's journal, *Reports of Explorations and Surveys to Ascertain the Most Practical and Economical Route for a Railroad from the Mississippi River to the Pacific Ocean.* Most notable among his sketches is a fine rendition of Cairook's house, with Cairook himself standing on the roof and two young boys playing a game of hoops below. Roof-sitting was quite common among the Mojave, and it was not uncommon to see as many as thirty people sitting on a roof at one time.

Lieutenant Whipple told the old chief of the imminent arrival of a railroad. The chief concluded that this would be beneficial to the tribe for trade purposes.

During their time in the village, the survey team replenished their supply of produce by trading with the Mojaves, who had experienced a bountiful harvest as a result of the spring overflow of the Colorado. Whipple asked Espaniole to assign a Mojave guide to the expedition temporarily. A tribal council was held, and Cairook was chosen to accompany the survey team, a likely choice because of his familiarity with the English language.

That afternoon, Cairook went looking for Olive. He found her working in her little garden near the chief's house. Empote-John slept peacefully in his little cradle close by. She stood up when he approached.

"I have come to say good-bye," he said.

"Where are you going?" she asked.

"I go with the white soldier and his men. I am their guide. They will pay me."

"What is this about white soldiers? Are they here in the village?" she asked, trying to hide her excitement.

"They say they are doing a survey for the *Americanos* in Washington. They want to build a railroad through our lands. My father thinks it will be good for trade, but I am not sure."

"How long will they be here?"

Cairook sensed her eagerness and said, "You must not go into the village. Stay out of sight. If the *Americanos* see you, they will tell the soldiers at the fort, and they will send many soldiers to kill us."

Olive thought about this. She looked down at her sleeping child.

"I will do as you wish."

"I must go now. There is much to do."

"Wait! When will you return?" she called after him.

"When my work is done," he said. Then he turned and walked away.

She watched him until he was out of sight.

Lieutenant Whipple gave Cairook several strings of white porcelain beads, a blue blanket, and a serape as payment for his services. At his own request, he was furnished with a dragoon's jacket. Of this he was most proud and, on cool mornings, he would stride out in front of the team wearing the jacket and a loincloth. This combination might have looked ridiculous on most men, but with his six-foot-six height and well proportioned body, he was most impressive.

The old chief's younger brother, Yara Tav, also accompanied the expedition as a guide. He was Cairook's uncle, but not much older than Cairook. In his report, Whipple refers to Yara Tav as "Iretaba," presumably because that is how it sounded to him. Lieutenant Joseph C. Ives, a member of Whipple's survey team, would lead another survey in 1857 and 1858 to determine the navigability of the Colorado River. In his *Report Upon the Colorado River of the West,* Ives also refers to Yara Tav as "Iretaba." Yara Tav received two shirts and some white beads for his service to the Whipple expedition.

Cairook and Yara Tav accompanied the expedition as far as the Mormon Road which leads to Los Angeles They were back within a few weeks.

Whipple's report states that Cairook and Yara Tav proved invaluable, as they were able to lead them to water sources and forage for their animals.

Chapter XXVIII
Bad Medicine

The Mojaves had a simple theory of medicine. Disease was divided into two categories, spiritual and physical. The physical was treated by wrapping the patient in blankets and placing him over the steam created by their medical leaves heated in water. For the treatment of their spiritual, or more malignant, diseases, the medicine men were employed. Any sickness that did not respond to the medical leaf treatment was considered dangerous and was referred to the medicine men.

In the summer of 1855, a malignant fever spread throughout the tribe. Several died. Members of the families of two of the sub-chiefs became ill, and the medicine men were called in. These "doctors" performed their "cures" by manipulations and wild contortions of their own bodies, accompanied by loud incantations and the shaking of gourd rattles over the sick. Their faces were painted black and white, giving them the appearance of supernatural deities reincarnated. They professed to be in league with the spirits of the departed, who guided them in all their curative rituals.

Two of them were called to the bed-side of the children of the sub-chiefs. They wailed, wrung their hands, and twisted their bodies into all manner of positions for several hours, all in vain. The children died.

The medicine men had lost several patients recently, and threats were beginning to follow them from house to house as their failures became known. After the death of these children of rank, the medicine men were accused of selling their souls to evil spirits for the purpose of bringing injury to the tribe. Vengeance was sworn upon them, and, aware of their danger, they hid themselves on the other side of the river. For several days, a search was conducted, but they could not be found. Friends and relatives protected them. But the sub-chiefs demanded revenge for the deaths of their children, and others who had lost family members joined them in their demands.

The chief gave orders for the arrest of the medicine men. They were found, arrested, and burned alive.

The Mojaves believed that when people died, they departed to a certain high hill in the western section of their territory. There, if they had been good and brave, they were free to pursue their dreams, free from the ills and pains of their life on earth. All cowardly Indians were tormented with hardships, sickness, and defeats. This hill, or hell, they never dared to visit, as it was inhabited by thousands of demons who would wreak vengeance upon mortals who dared to intrude on this temple of horrors.

Chapter XXIX
Lorenzo's Obsession

After his recovery, Lorenzo remained at Fort Yuma for nearly three months. Dr. Hewitt had taken a fatherly interest in him, and after listening to conversations between Dr. Hewitt and some of the officers, Lorenzo understood why he had decided to resign his post as the fort's surgeon. It was the consensus of the officers that Major Heintzelman was a thoroughly disagreeable man.

In early June of 1851, the army decided that Fort Yuma could no longer be provisioned from San Diego and ordered the fort closed. All of the men stationed at the fort were transferred to San Diego, with the exception of twelve soldiers who remained to guard the ferry crossing. Dr. Hewitt and Lorenzo traveled to San Diego with the transferred troops. When they arrived in San Diego, Dr. Hewitt and Lorenzo boarded a ship to San Francisco, where they arrived on June 26, 1851. Lorenzo remained in San Francisco with the Hewitt family until they left for the East Coast. During this time, Dr. Hewitt continued to do everything he could to help Lorenzo obtain information about the location of his sisters. He maintained contact with the men he knew at the fort, and they had promised to search for information among friendly Indians. On a cool, foggy morning, two weeks before he left, Dr. Hewitt called Lorenzo to his study.

"Lorenzo, come in and sit down, lad."

Lorenzo was apprehensive. The doctor was not his usual ebullient self. He sat down in a chair facing Dr. Hewitt, who sat behind his cluttered desk.

"As you know, we are leaving California and moving back to Connecticut. You are welcome to join us, but I know you would not be happy as long as there is any hope of locating your two sisters. I have made arrangements for you to live with a good friend of mine. His name is Walter Johnson. He owns a wholesale business here in

San Francisco and has agreed to employ you. I have explained to Mr. Johnson that you are most anxious to find your sisters, and he has agreed to do all he can to help you in that pursuit."

After Dr. Hewitt left for the East Coast, Lorenzo became despondent. At times, he resolved to arm himself, take provisions, and go in search of his sisters alone, but reason prevailed. He realized this would accomplish nothing and probably lead to his death.

He soon found that the tasks assigned to him in Mr. Johnson's wholesale firm were beyond his years and strength. He seriously injured himself by lifting and was compelled to leave. He later regretted this, as he found unemployment miserable.

He took to wandering in the hills surrounding San Francisco to get away from the raucous hordes of gold seekers that constantly passed through the city on their way to make their fortunes in the gold country. Lorenzo was an Illinois farm boy accustomed to hard work. He could not relate to the get-rich-quick mentality of these frantic men who swarmed over the city like a plague of locusts. They spoke a language all their own that was foreign to Lorenzo. They used terms like *sluice box, hydraulic mining, assay office,* and *diggin's.*

Lorenzo was constantly tormented by thoughts of his sisters and what terrible fate they might be enduring. Three years passed. Some of the time he worked in the mines, and occasionally, he found work in the city. When a stranger asked him why he was so sad, he would tell them the story of the massacre and the capture of his two sisters. Some would be extremely moved and offer to help him find his sisters. Others found his story incredible.

He decided to go to Los Angeles, where he hoped to obtain some knowledge of conditions in the area of Fort Yuma. In October of 1854, he left for Los Angeles and resolved to stay there until he gained some knowledge of his sisters' whereabouts, if it took a lifetime.

In Los Angeles, he found emigrants who had recently passed through Fort Yuma and some who had spent time in the same stopping places he and his family had. He questioned them for any rumors they might have heard with regard to Olive and Mary Ann. He wrote letters to the fort on a regular basis. Since the Gadsden purchase in 1853, the

New Mexico territory was made part of the United States, so Lorenzo saw no reason why the fort commander could not send soldiers into the Apache country to rescue his sisters.

He worked by the month to earn a living and spent his free time planning his exploration of the regions surrounding Fort Yuma and beyond. Another year passed, and in the spring of 1855, he met several emigrants who had come by the same trail, but they knew nothing, except what they had learned at Fort Yuma regarding the fate of the Oatman family.

One group of emigrants told Lorenzo that they had met a Mr. Henry Grinnell, the fort carpenter, who told them he knew of the massacre of the Oatman family and the captivity of the girls and that he intended to do all in his power to recover them. Grinnell had told them that their brother, Lorenzo, who had been left for dead by the Indians, was now alive in Los Angeles and that he knew this because Lorenzo had sent a letter to Fort Yuma urging them to rescue his sisters. This carpenter, Mr. Henry Grinnell, also stated that he had been making inquiries among the Yuma Indians concerning the captive girls. This gave Lorenzo a bit of hope, but he continued to try to enlist companions to accompany him on a rescue mission.

Lorenzo tried, on several occasions, to organize a search party from among acquaintances, but after all preparations had been made, the volunteers backed out on some pretext or another. This had occurred several times, but he was not discouraged. The recovery of his sisters was his primary aim in life, but he had learned a valuable lesson in human nature: men did not travel across the desert to hunt captives among the Indians.

Several parties of men were organized late in 1855 to hunt gold on the Colorado River, about a hundred miles from San Bernardino. Lorenzo joined some of these parties with the promise of several men to extend their search for gold to a hunt for his sisters. On one of these expeditions, he succeeded in going beyond and to the north of Fort Yuma, but he could not convince his companions to enter the Apache country. They would say that his sisters were probably dead and that it was useless to search for them. He joined a survey party, hoping they would venture into Apache country, but they would not.

While Lorenzo was away on one of his expeditions to the Colorado River, an article appeared in the *Los Angeles Star* on January 5, 1856. It read as follows:

> "A man by the name of Frank, a member of Captain Washburn's survey team just in from the plains, said that he had seen Olive Oatman during the summer of 1855 and that she was living among the Mojave and married to one of the chiefs of that tribe."

This item was picked up by the *San Francisco Chronicle* and appeared in that newspaper on January 19, 1856. Lorenzo had not seen either of these articles.

Chapter XXX
The Ransom

In 1855, a full complement of men was again transferred to Fort Yuma, including several officers and soldiers who had been there in 1851 at the time of the massacre. Commander Heintzelman was no longer in charge. Major George Thomas was interim commander and was succeeded in 1855 by Brevet Lieutenant Colonel Martin Burke, who had distinguished himself in the battle of Molino del Rey during the Mexican-American War. He was a good officer and was well-respected by his soldiers.

On April 22nd, 1855, a letter was received at Fort Yuma from F. A. Rondstadt, sent from Colorado. It read as follows:

Major George Thomas, Esq., Commander, Fort Yuma

By request of Captain Garcia, a Mexican officer, I address these few lines to you.

From information given by Capt. Garcia, the gentleman killed by the Mojave Indians in 1851 on the Gila was Mr. Oatman, and the two girls are still in their possession.

Last evening, when I got home, I was told that a Mojave Indian by the name of Francisco was at my place yesterday when I was at Fort Yuma, and he is now at a visit on the opposite bank of the river. If he is sought and obtained, I believe you would acquire true information about the unhappy captives.

Respectfully, your most obedient servant Frederico A. Rondstadt

While some of the statements in the letter were incorrect; e.g., that the Oatmans were killed by the Mojave and that Francisco was a Mojave Indian (he was a Yuma), the fact that the captive girls were among the Mojave was correct, although Mary Ann was already dead by the time the letter was written.

Henry Grinnell, the fort carpenter, who had vowed to find and rescue Olive and Mary Ann, saw this letter and thought that the Indian referred to might be Francisco, a Yuma, with whom he had struck up a friendship in order to gain information. So far, he had learned nothing.

However, one night toward the end of January, 1856, Francisco managed to elude the fort guard and came to Mr. Grinnell's tent after he had retired. Grinnell awoke, drew his pistol, and demanded, "Who's there?"

"Francisco, the Yuma."

Mr. Grinnell recognized his voice and lowered his pistol. He lit a lantern and held it up to examine Francisco's face.

"What brings you here this hour of the night?"

"I only come in to talk a little," he answered.

After a long silence, he said, *"Carpentero,* what is this you say so much about two *Americanos* among the Indians?"

"I said that there are two girls among the Mojave or Apaches, and you know it, and we know that you know it."

Grinnell then reached over to a small table and picked up a copy of the *Los Angeles Star.*

"Listen, I will read you what the *Americanos* are saying and thinking about."

He then read the article that had been published at the insistence of Lorenzo, translating it into Spanish, which Francisco understood. It contained the report brought in by Mr. Rowlit calling for help. The article also stated that a large number of men were ready to undertake the rescue of the captives at once, if means were furnished. Keeping his eyes on the paper, he added a few comments of his own.

"If the captives are not delivered in so many days, there will be five million men thrown around the mountains inhabited by the Indians, and they will annihilate every last one of them if they do not give up the white captives."

Francisco listened with complete attention. After a short silence, he said, "I know where there is one white girl among the Mojave—there were two, but one is dead."

"When did you find out she was there?"

"I have just found out tonight."

"Did you know it before?"

"Well, not long. Me just come in, you know. Me know now she is there among the Mojave."

Grinnell was not fully satisfied. There had been apprehension at the fort of some trouble from the Yumas, and Grinnell was suspicious that some murderous scheme was being concocted and this was a ruse to deceive him. Grinnell told Francisco to stay in his tent for the night. Francisco then told Grinnell that if Commander Burke would give him authority, he would go and bring the girl to the fort. Grinnell did not sleep that night.

Early the next morning, they went to see the commander. For some time, Commander Burke was skeptical. He thought it might be a scheme originated by Francisco for his personal gain and did not believe he would bring the girl in.

"You give me four blankets and some beads, and I will bring her here in just twenty days, when the sun be right over here." Francisco pointed about forty-five degrees above the western horizon.

Grinnell pleaded with Commander Burke.

"Please let him go, sir. You may bill the entire cost of the outfit to my own account."

The commander reluctantly consented. A letter was written, and Francisco, with a brother and two others, left for the Mojave village on the eighth of February, 1856.

As the weeks slipped by with no word from Francisco, Henry Grinnell became the brunt of many jokes for trusting an Indian.

Chapter XXXI
The Tribal Council

One day in the middle of February 1856, Olive was grinding mesquite near the door of her hut as her son played close by and her newborn slept peacefully in his little cradle. A young boy came running toward her. He was excited and breathless.

"The Yuma crier, Francisco, is on his way here. He is coming to take you away to the whites."

Olive was stunned. When she recovered her composure, she began to suspect that this was just another cruel hoax concocted by lazy idlers to torment her and amuse themselves. However, in a few moments, the report was circulating on good authority. One of the sub-chiefs came in and said that a Yuma Indian named Francisco was now on his way with orders to secure her immediate release and safe return to Fort Yuma. Olive knew there were whites at Fort Yuma, but did not know how far it was. She also knew that runners, or criers, kept up a steady traffic between the Yumas and the Mojaves and thought that perhaps this was how the Yumas had learned of her presence in the Mojave village.

Before long, the report had spread throughout the entire valley with astonishing speed, and a crowd had gathered in the village. Chief Espaniole convened a council meeting attended by the sub-chiefs and other tribal leaders. Espaniole had been a tall, strongly-built man and was still an imposing figure. He was active and generally happy. He possessed a mildness of disposition and seriousness very rare among Indians. He ruled a council with an ease and authority that few men can command. This council would be a challenge, even to him, as it was more a convening of wild maniacs in a state of high excitement.

Olive was not permitted to attend the council, so she inquired of some of the women who passed by whether the report was true or false and, if there was a message, who had sent it. She asked those she met what they thought and how the tribe was reacting to this development, but none would discuss it. She wished she could ask Cairook, but he was sequestered with the council, and she would not see him until it had adjourned. Though Olive was not able to elicit any information, it was certain that she, and the demand for her release, was the subject of this council meeting.

In the midst of all the uproar and confusion, the approach of Francisco, the Yuma, was announced. The debate suddenly ceased, and everyone stared at Francisco as he strode boldly toward the *ramada* where the council meeting was being held. Some of the Mojaves were sullen and would not speak to him, while some were indifferent and indicated that they did not care about Olive, saying *"Degee, degee, ontoa, ontoa."* Others were angry and wanted to bar him from the council and drive him away at once.

Olive saw Francisco enter the lodge, and she was simultaneously accosted by two Indians and told to go into her hogan and stay there. She was shut up with her two children and unprotected. She could still hear the commotion outside. She began to pray, as she knew her life hung in the balance. Her worst fear was that the Mojaves would become enraged and inflamed by the fact that the whites were now aware of Olive's presence among them. The torture and death of the Cocopah captive Nowereha and the burning alive of the medicine men were still fresh in her mind. They wouldn't dare do that to the wife of a sub-chief—or would they? She had seen them whipped into a frenzy before and knew they were capable of anything if provoked. That night, she trembled with fear and could not sleep. Cairook did not come home.

For three days and nights, the noisy council deliberated. Olive wondered what Cairook was thinking as he sat in the council listening to all of these arguments that would determine his wife's fate.

Olive still did not know how the whites had come to know of her whereabouts or who had sent the demand for her release. She wondered whether the demand had been written or oral and who had issued it. She saw and heard enough to know they would not let her go free. The attitude of the Indians toward her had become hostile and resentful. Even her mother-in-law, Aespaneo, seemed cool toward her. She began to fear for her life.

As deliberations progressed, Olive became aware that all efforts to rescue her had come to an abrupt halt. It was obvious to Olive that some dreadful fear was galling and tormenting the Mojaves. She overheard some expressing their fear that the whites would make good their threats against the tribe, as related by Francisco. She saw and heard enough to know they would not let her go free.

Olive had been forbidden to speak to Francisco. Finally, the council came to an end with a positive and preemptive refusal to liberate the "captive" and a resolution to send Francisco away with a warning not to return under penalty of torture. When the council was finally adjourned, Cairook returned to their hogan and embraced her.

"You will stay here with me," he said emphatically.

"What of Francisco and the demand for my release?"

"Francisco has gone to tell the whites that you chose to remain here with your husband and children. He has been told not to return under penalty of torture."

"But who made the demand for my release?" she asked.

"The fort commander signed the letter. Francisco has told us that the white man's newspaper is saying that if you are not released, many soldiers will come and destroy all of the Mojaves and Yumas they can find."

She thought about this for a moment, her face reflecting the conflict within.

"If I do not go, the soldiers will come and kill us all—you, me, our two sons, your parents, Topeka—everyone." Olive burst into tears. She regretted that anything had been done to effect her rescue. She did not sleep that night, and although Cairook tried to comfort her, she sobbed, even as she nursed the baby.

That night, Francisco withdrew to the other side of the river. It soon became apparent that he had not given up. He implored the principal Mojaves on that side of the Colorado to reconsider and retract the resolution they had reached that day. All that night, he warned them of the destruction they would bring down upon the tribe and tried to convince them that it was for their sake alone that he desired to take the captive to the fort.

If all else failed, Francisco was prepared to steal Olive away in the darkness. In the morning, he made preparations to leave. This was a ruse to cover his real intentions. Some of the councilmen who had spoken with him the night before came to him and prevailed upon him to go back to the village with them. They promised that they would do everything in their power to persuade the chief and tribe to yield to his demands and let the captive go. They said they were not prepared to subject themselves and the tribe to the wrath of the white soldiers for a mere woman.

About noon the next day, Olive saw Francisco come into the village with a large number of Mojaves. She trembled with fear and anxiety but was, at the same time, relieved that the terrible waiting would now be over. After all this turmoil, she plainly saw that she could no longer live among the Mojaves. They would see her as the cause of their fear and disruption of peace. Now that the whites knew of her whereabouts, she would be closely and constantly watched. If the soldiers came, she would be seen as the cause of the tribe's annihilation. Even if she survived the attack, the Mojaves would kill her for bringing down the white man's wrath upon them.

Francisco and his entourage came directly to the house of the chief. The chief refused to receive them. However, after a brief consultation with the members of his cabinet, he yielded. The sub-chiefs were called and, with Francisco, they were again in council. The criers ran about the village gathering the tribe.

Olive was permitted to attend this council. Soon, everyone was speaking at once, and there was great confusion which the chief found difficult to control. Speakers were continuously interrupted, and turmoil erupted. Tempers were unleashed, and at times, threatened to become violent. Olive later wrote,

> It seemed, during that night, at several stages of the debate, that a fight was inevitable. Speeches were made, which, judging from their gestures and motions,

as well as from what I could understand, were full of the most impassioned eloquence. I looked closely at Francisco and realized that I had seen him about three months before when he had visited the chief. I noticed that he now held a letter in his hand and I asked him to let me see it. Toward morning, it was handed to me. I took it, and the council demanded I read it and give them the contents of it. I examined it carefully. I had not seen writing for five years. On the outside, in large letters, it said:

"Francisco, a Yuma Indian, going to the Mojaves."

Olive opened it slowly, her hand trembling so she could hardly read the words. The council was hushed, and all eyes were fastened on her face. She examined it for a long time, trying to make sense of it. It said:

Francisco, Yuma Indian, bearer of this, goes to the Mojave Nation to obtain a white woman there, named Olivia. It is desirable that she should come to this post, or send her reasons why she does not wish to come.

Martin Burke, Lieutenant Colonel Commanding, Head Quarters, Fort Yuma, Cal'a
27th January, 1856

The council now began to threaten Olive to give them the contents of the letter. She hesitated, not knowing whether to give them exactly what was written. Cairook had told her that Francisco maintained that the whites knew where she was and that they were already arming a sufficient number of men to surround the whole Indian nation and that they intended to destroy them all, unless they gave up their white captive. Francisco had also told them that the soldiers would kill him and all the Mojaves and Yumas they could find if he didn't bring her back. He said that it was out of mercy for his own tribe and for the Mojave that he had come.

Now they turned to Olive. She then told them what was in it, adding that the *Americanos* would send a large army to destroy the Yumas and Mojaves and all the Indians they could find, unless she returned with Francisco. Her audience was hushed. Not a sound was heard.

Olive learned that they had been telling Francisco that she did not wish to go to the whites. As soon as they heard and understood the contents of the letter, everyone began to yell at once. Some said Olive should be killed and that Francisco should report that she was dead. Others flatly refused to let her go and shouted that the whites could not hurt them. Others were in favor of letting her go at once.

Through all of this, Francisco was bold, calm, and determined. He answered all their questions and objections with the tact and cunning of a pure Indian.

As for Olive, she knew she must hold her tongue and keep her emotions hidden during the remainder of the pow-wow, as she was terrified of inciting the wrath of the council. The sun was now beginning to rise in the east, and the council continued to deliberate on the life or death of their captive. The chief told Francisco and Olive to leave the council. A short time later, the chief called them back and told them, with reluctance, that the decision had been to let the captive go.

Olive could no longer control her emotions. She burst into tears as relief flooded through her. The council looked on, not knowing whether she was happy or sad. She later learned that the chief had accused Francisco of coming to take her from the Mojaves so that she could become a slave to the Yumas. This had incited Francisco's anger, and he had boldly told them what he thought of them and that they could keep their captive, but would be sorry for it in the end.

When it was finally determined that Olive should go, the chief said he would send his daughter, Topeka, with two Mojave guides to insure that Olive was delivered to the whites and that Topeka would be returned safely.

That night, Olive and Cairook sat staring at the fire at the door of their hogan. In a corner of the room, their little faces illuminated by the flickering firelight, their two little boys slept peacefully in their blankets. The only sound was the crackling of the fire as the silence stretched out interminably. Finally, Olive spoke.

"Your father has told me I must go. He thinks that Commander Burke will send the soldiers to destroy us if I do not return with Francisco."

"I do not want you to go, but I must obey my father and protect my people. If Francisco speaks the truth, we will all be killed unless you return to the whites. My father has spoken. You must do as he says."

Olive looked at his face. He remained stoic, as always. His strong features were impassive, but his eyes betrayed his sadness as he continued to stare at the dwindling flames.

"Will I be permitted to take my sons? They are all I have, and the baby is still suckling."

He did not look at her, but remained transfixed by the fire.

"They will stay here with their own people. I have told you how the whites treat half-breeds. I will find a nursing mother for our baby. He will not go hungry. He is the grandson of the chief. Any squaw would be proud to suckle him."

Olive's face revealed her pain. She lowered her eyes as tears streamed down her cheeks.

"I wish they had never found me. How did they know I was here?"

"What does it matter? They know."

"But I have no family. They are all dead. You and our sons are my family now. Your people are my people. Please, don't send me away."

He stood and held out his hand.

"Come, we have one last night together. Let us not waste it."

She took his hand and stood up. Then they walked to their blankets for the last time.

Olive woke just before dawn. She nursed her baby for the last time, trying to hold back her tears. She wrapped him in his little blanket, kissed him, and placed him in his cradle. Then she knelt and kissed Empote-John, careful not to wake him. She dressed hurriedly, rolled her meager belongings in a blanket, and, with a last look at Cairook as he slept, left the hogan that he had built for her.

She walked hurriedly toward the chief's house, where Topeka stood waiting for her at the door. She gave Olive a corn cake to eat and took along some mesquite mush for the journey. Before they left, they went to Mary Ann's grave. Olive said a prayer and whispered, "Goodbye." She was saddened by having to leave Mary Ann's remains behind. She feared the Mojaves might exhume and burn them, as they had threatened to do in the past. Topeka sensed her concerns and attempted to calm her fears.

"As long as I am alive, I will not permit your sister's grave to be disturbed."

Somewhat assured, Olive thanked Topeka, and together, they walked toward the river to meet Francisco and the others.

As the little group prepared to leave, a small crowd gathered. Many expressed sadness, especially some of the children Olive had cared for. When more people began to arrive, Olive grew apprehensive. Some were angry and resented her leaving. Others demanded that she give back the strings of beads and red fabric that had been given to her and Mary Ann in appreciation for their singing. This she did in order to avoid conflict. She did manage to hide a few mesquite berries in her bark skirt, and these she kept for the rest of her life.

Topeka chastised the belligerent ones, and they retreated a bit, not wanting to provoke the chief's daughter. Then Francisco gave the order to start. They quickly crossed the river and did not slow down until they were well away from the village. Olive continued to feel uneasy until they had passed beyond the voices of the dissidents. She had been in captivity for five years and ten days.

Olive was relieved that Cairook had chosen to stay at home with the children. It was not in his nature to display his emotions in public.

She felt guilty about substantiating Francisco's claims that the soldiers would annihilate the Indians if she did not return, but she was not willing to risk the lives of her little family in the event that he was telling the truth. As for Francisco, he was only repeating what Henry Grinnell had read to him from the white man's newspaper.

Chapter XXXII
Mixed Emotions

They traveled three hundred and fifty miles over rough terrain, and several times Olive and her guides had to swim and float in the ice-cold, swollen river which rushed swiftly along, propelled by early spring runoff.

One night, after the others had gone to sleep, Olive and Topeka sat by the dying embers of the little campfire. Olive was crying softly. Topeka moved closer to her, wrapping her blanket about Olive's shoulders. Finally, Topeka whispered, "You should be happy you are going back to your people. My brother is hurt, but he will not show weakness. He will be strong and perhaps find another to share his blankets, tend his fires, and care for his children."

"They are my children too, Topeka. The thought of my boys calling another woman 'mother' is more than I can bear. You say I am going back to my people, but the whites at the fort are not my people. My white family is dead. You, Cairook, and my little boys are my family. Why must I leave you to live among strangers?"

"Olive, you know what will happen to the tribe if you are not brought to the fort. My father has told me of the white soldiers' threat to annihilate us. I don't want you to go, but I see no other way. Surely you do not want to see your sons killed by the soldiers. I promise you I will care for them as if they were my own."

"I will go to the fort and tell Commander Burke that I want to go back to my children. If he sees that I have not been harmed and that I am choosing to return to the Mojaves of my own free will, I am sure he will let me go without consequences to the tribe."

"I will wait until you have spoken to the commander before I leave."

Olive stood and looked down at Topeka.

"I have no more tears, my sister. I will sleep now."

143

Topeka stood and spread the blankets on the sand. They soon fell into an exhausted sleep.

The next morning, they awoke at daybreak, shared a mesquite cake, and, when everyone was ready to leave, resumed their journey.

Topeka, with an affection that had increased with every year of their association, showed more concern for Olive's welfare than her own. During the entire journey, Topeka carried the roll of blankets that she shared with Olive every night. When floating down the river, she skillfully held the roll of blankets above her head to keep it dry. She seemed very anxious and concerned that something might occur to prevent Olive from reaching her destination. It would take eight days to complete the arduous journey from the Mojave village to Fort Yuma.

As the weeks passed, Mr. Grinnell, or *Carpentero,* as he was called by the Indians, had become the brunt of many a joke at the fort. The men asked him if he thought his blankets and beads were gone forever.

"Where's your trusty Francisco now?" they teased. "Maybe you should send another Indian after the blankets." They laughed and hooted.

On the twentieth day, around noon, three Yuma Indians came to the fort and asked to see *"Carpentero."* They were shown to his tent and went in. It was February 22, 1856.

"Carpentero, Francisco is coming," they said.

Grinnell bounded to his feet.

"Is the girl with them?" he asked.

They laughed.

"Francisco will come when the sun be right over there." They pointed in the direction specified by Francisco.

Grinnell ran out of the tent and stood watching the river down below for some time. Finally, two Indians and two females dressed in bark skirts came down to the ferry on the opposite side of the river. He ran toward the river, shouting loudly, "They have come. The captive girl is here."

Soon, men began running from the fort to meet and welcome the captive. Then the officers' wives and the fort's cook came running out to get a look at her.

When she came within sight of the fort and saw all the people awaiting her arrival on the opposite bank, Olive tried to bury herself in the sand to cover her semi-nudity. As soon as her predicament was made known, one of the officers' wives sent her a dress, the best she had. Another dress was produced for Topeka. The girls slipped the dresses over their heads, each helping the other with the buttons. They dropped their bark skirts on the sand. Topeka picked them up and carried them along with her blanket roll.

Unaccustomed to long dresses, Olive and Topeka felt awkward and kept tripping on the hem until they got the knack of lifting the front of the skirt slightly to facilitate walking. When Olive was asked her name, she replied, "Olive."

Chapter XXXIII
Civilization

She was tattooed and so tanned from exposure to the sun that some of the men doubted that she was white, but on closer examination, her blue eyes confirmed it. She appeared to be in shock, and for a couple of days, she spoke very little, having all but forgotten her native language.

Amid long, enthusiastic cheering and the booming of canon, Miss Olive was presented to Commander Burke by Francisco. Joy and enthusiasm prevailed, and those skeptics who had chided Henry Grinnell slapped him on the back and apologized. The Yumas soon gathered in large numbers and joined in on the general rejoicing. Their heavy, shrill voices and wild dancing fairly shook the earth. Later, Francisco told Commander Burke that he had been compelled to pay more for the captive than was originally allotted. He had promised the Mojave chief a horse, and his daughter was now present to see that this promise was fulfilled. He said the chief's son, Cairook, would be here in a few days to receive the horse.

The commander promised he would give the chief's son a good horse. Then each of the officers donated money for the purchase of a horse for Francisco in gratitude for his brave act. Commander Burke gave a speech in the presence of the Yuma tribe, commending Francisco for performing a heroic act for which the gratitude of the whites would follow him and one that might save his tribe and the Mojaves much trouble and many lives.

Francisco was later promoted and became a *Tie* of his tribe and, with characteristic pride and haughtiness of bearing, showed the capabilities of the Indian to appreciate honors and preferment. He looked with disdain and contempt upon his peers and treated them accordingly in the presence of the whites.

Olive was soon told that her brother, Lorenzo, was still alive and that he had never given up hope of finding her. She was incredulous. The last time she had seen him, he was being dragged, beaten and bleeding, to the rocks on the edge of a steep precipice. She was sure he was dead. When the details of his survival and medical treatment at Fort Yuma were made known to her, she finally accepted that he was truly alive.

Commander Burke placed Olive in the care of Sarah Bowman, known as "The Great Western," a nurse who had shown great valor during the Mexican-American War. "The Great Western" was the name bestowed on Sarah by the troops because she stood over six feet tall and reminded them of a steamship by the same name. She was now in charge of the officers' mess at the fort. She ordered food and supplies through the fort's commissary supply sergeant and saw to it that the officers' meals were properly prepared and served in a timely manner.

At first glance, Sarah appeared a bit rough around the edges. Her hair was always slightly askew, and loose ends fell about her face in unruly wisps. Outdoors, she wore an old, battered cavalry hat, a souvenir from her Mexican- American War days. Her voice was gritty and loud. But she had a good heart and bustled about Olive, solicitous of her comfort.

In the past, Sarah had run afoul of Major Heintzelman when he was fort commander. Fort Yuma was not considered a choice assignment. The summers were particularly oppressive due to the extreme desert heat. Sarah took it upon herself to do everything possible to keep the soldiers' morale high by supplying delicious meals, clean laundry, and other "creature comforts."

Unfortunately for Sarah, one of these "creature comforts" was the procurement of prostitutes. The Mexican women who worked in the fort's laundry by day were only too happy to earn some extra cash at night. When Major Heintzelman discovered her little enterprise, he called her into his office and chastised her for a full hour. When she'd had enough, she told him to "mind his own damn business" and flounced out of his office, leaving him to fume and sputter in solitude.

Sarah's accommodations were very basic. She lived in a large tent adjoining the officers' mess. She had hung army blankets to divide the tent into sections. The largest was a living area furnished with two flimsy chairs, a table, and a makeshift cabinet containing a few dishes, two tin cups, a coffee pot, a cast iron cooking pot, and a frying pan. Another section contained an army cot and a small washstand with a chamber pot. A very small area contained a straw mattress which sat directly on the canvas floor, an empty biscuit tin, a coffee can, and a wooden crate stood on end, with a small center divider providing a shelf. A fourth section contained a large, metal tub and an old coat rack with two flour sacks hanging from it. Olive stared at the tub in disbelief.

Sarah ordered two soldiers to heat two large kettles of water on the big cook stove in the officers' mess. They emptied the kettles of scalding water into the tub, then hauled in some cool water and added it to the tub. Sarah provided homemade soap and a washcloth.

Within two hours after her arrival, Olive was soaking in a warm, sudsy bath. She luxuriated in the warm, fragrant water for a good half-hour. After her soak, Sarah shampooed her hair with a strong disinfectant, explaining as she scrubbed, "This'll take care of any small critters that might be runnin' loose in yer lovely long locks."

When Olive had dried herself with the two flour sacks, Sarah helped her into a freshly laundered dress which had been donated by one of the officers' wives. Then, to Olive's surprise, Sarah produced a tiny bottle of cologne from an old, battered medical case that she kept under her cot. It was obvious to Olive that this was Sarah's most prized possession, as she handled it as if it were a precious diamond and sparingly dabbed a small amount behind each of Olive's ears. Olive was overwhelmed by Sarah's kindness.

"Thank you, Sarah," she said in halting English.

Sarah beamed. "You're more than welcome, honey. I think you're beginnin' to remember how to speak American."

That evening, she was invited to join the officers and their wives for dinner. She appeared, bathed, combed, and scented, at their table, and everyone agreed she was a very attractive young woman despite the tattoo on her chin. She was escorted to her seat by Sarah Bowman, who beamed with pride over her transformation.

When Olive beheld the abundance of food that appeared on her plate, she could not believe her eyes. For the past five years, she had existed on such a meager diet that it was more than she could comprehend. She ate slowly and reverently, savoring each morsel.

Topeka, despite the fact that she was the daughter of the Mojave chief, was assigned a small room adjacent to the stables, where she slept on a rough palette with her own bedroll.

One of the men brought her a plate of food from the enlisted men's mess, and she ate every scrap. The next morning, Topeka came to Sarah's tent.

"Did you speak to the commander, Olive?" she asked.

"Topeka, you will never believe this, but my brother, Lorenzo, is alive. The commander has sent a dispatch to a newspaper in California saying that I am at Fort Yuma. He expects that my brother will be on his way very soon. I can't wait to see him. I was sure he was dead, but he survived and was found by friends from our wagon train. Oh, Topeka, it's a miracle."

"Then you will stay to see your brother. I am happy for you, but I am sad that you will not be returning with me."

"Please try to understand, Topeka. Mr.Grinnell, the fort carpenter who paid for my ransom, has told me that Lorenzo often writes to Commander Burke for news of me and Mary Ann. He has never given up hope of finding us. I could not disappoint him now. He does not know about Mary Ann, but I will have to tell him."

"I would do the same if it were my brother. If you ever wish to return, come to the fort and ask the commander to send a Yuma runner for me. I will come for you. Now I must go. Goodbye, Olive."

They hugged each other and shed many tears.

"Topeka, my sister, I will always be grateful to you for taking Mary Ann and me from the Apaches. If not for you, I would not be alive today."

"It was my father who gave me permission and the goods to trade for you."

"But if you had not begged him to do so, it would never have happened."

She smiled. "I had my own selfish reasons, Olive. I wanted two little sisters. My older sisters have families of their own, and no time for me."

They hugged each other a final time, and as Topeka turned to walk away, Olive called out, "Please take care of my boys, Topeka." Tears welled up in her eyes.

"They will be fine, Olive. They will get much love from my whole family, and Cairook is a good father."

Olive watched her until she joined her two guides and slowly disappeared from view. Then she broke down and cried for a long time, not only for Topeka, but for Cairook and her two little boys.

In the days that followed while they awaited Lorenzo's arrival, Sarah told Olive how frustrated she had been when Heintzelman refused to send troops to search for her and Mary Ann.

"He was a prissy little jackass who was too preoccupied with his own interests. He forgot that he took an oath to protect the emigrants. He was too busy collecting big fares to ferry their wagons across the river," she said.

She told Olive that he had liked to ridicule Dr. Le Conte by referring to him as "Doctor Bugs."

"The fact is, Dr. Le Conte had studied medicine. So he was a medical doctor as well as a well-respected entomologist," she said. "When he gave Heintzelman the letter from your father, Heintzelman did nothing. When he finally sent two soldiers out, they found your family dead. If he had sent six soldiers as soon as he got the letter, they might have been able to catch up with you and the Apaches before you got to their village."

All of this was news to Olive, but it was sad news because everything might have turned out differently if Major Heintzelman had acted promptly.

A few days later, Cairook arrived to claim his horse. It was a fine animal, one of the best in the fort's stable, but it was small compensation for the loss of his wife, the mother of his children. Commander Burke ordered his soldiers to be on their guard while Cairook was at the fort, as he was afraid that the chief's son might attempt to take Olive back to the Mojaves.

Leaving nothing to chance, Commander Burke summoned Sarah to his office.

"Keep a careful watch on Miss Oatman. If the chief's son attempts to take her with him, I will face a severe reprimand from my superiors and the press will have a field day."

"Don't worry, commander, I'll stay on her like a tick on a hog's back," she replied.

Chapter XXXIV
The Reunion

In December, 1855, Lorenzo had been successful in recruiting five men who agreed to join him in the search for his sisters. They spent several weeks south and west of Fort Yuma and had returned to San Bernardino to buy provisions for a trip further north.

While in San Bernardino, Lorenzo received a letter from Ira Thomson in El Monte. The Thompsons now ran a small hotel there which was a stopping point for emigrants and travelers from the east. The letter stated that a Mr. Rowlit had just arrived in El Monte after having spent some time at Fort Yuma. While there, he had learned that Mr. Henry Grinnell, the fort carpenter, had been gathering information from the Yuma Indians, a tribe friendly with the Mojaves. One of the Yumas had told Grinnell that there were two white girls among the Mojaves. The Yuma said these captives had been part of a family attacked and murdered by the Apaches and that the Apaches had sold the captive girls to the Mojaves.

When Lorenzo read this, the tears ran freely down his face. He thought of little Mary Ann, who would be thirteen now, and Olive, who would be nineteen now.

Could they still be alive? Is there a chance I might see them again? These questions dominated his thoughts.

The next day, Lorenzo reached El Monte at seven AM after traveling all night .He met Mr. Rowlit, and he corroborated the contents of his letter. Lorenzo prepared a statement of the facts and sent them to the *Los Angeles Star.* The editor published these facts, accompanied by some well-timed and stirring remarks. This awakened the community, and there was an outpouring of sympathy and many letters to the editor.

While Lorenzo was staying with Susan and David Lewis at El Monte, a Mr. Black came to town from the east by way of Fort Yuma.

He stated that two girls were among the Mojaves and that the chief had offered them to the officers at the fort for a very nominal price, but that Commander Burke had refused to make the purchase. Lorenzo knew nothing of this until he read it in the *Los Angeles Star.* However, he later learned that Mr. Black was well known in El Monte and had a reputation for exaggeration. Those who knew him reserved judgment until the information could be verified by a reliable authority.

The editor of the *Star* had published Black's report with the best of intentions, but when it reached Fort Yuma, it created a sensation. Commander Burke sent a letter to the editor vehemently denying the truthfulness of Mr. Black's claims. Accompanying the letter was a statement confirming the existence of a report at the fort from reliable sources that the two girls were among the Mojaves, but no offer had been made to deliver them to the fort on any terms. As per Commander Burke's request, the editor published it.

During this time, Lorenzo had drawn up a petition with a large number of signatures which he sent to the governor of California, J. Neely Johnson, asking for men and provisions to go and rescue his captive sisters. He received a reply from the governor stating that it was not is his power to grant Lorenzo's request, but he suggested that Lorenzo contact the Department of Indian Affairs in Washington, D.C. Lorenzo drew up a letter to the Department of Indian Affairs stating the facts and attaching the petition. He delivered it to the office at the steamer landing to be forwarded to Washington.

Two days later, he was working in the woods a good distance from El Monte when his friend, Jesse Lowe, rode up to him and, without speaking, handed him a copy of the *Los Angeles Star,* pointing to an article on the front page. Lorenzo took it from his hand and read the following:

An American Woman Rescued from the Indians

A woman giving her name as Miss Olive Oatman has been recently rescued from the Mojaves and is now at Fort Yuma.

When Lorenzo recovered from his shock, he mounted his horse and went immediately to Los Angeles. He went to the *Los Angeles Star* and asked to see the editor. The editor had a letter which he had received from Commander Burke at Fort Yuma, stating that a young woman calling herself Olive Oatman had been recently brought to the fort by a Yuma Indian who had ransomed her from the Mojave tribe.

Commander Burke further stated that Olive had been informed of her brother's survival of the attack on their family. He requested that the editor locate Lorenzo and notify him of the rescue of his sister.

Lorenzo asked to see the letter. When he read the facts concerning Olive, he was completely overcome. He saw no mention of Mary Ann and immediately concluded that she had died among the savages, either by disease or cruelty.

Lorenzo was without money or means to get to the fort, but friends came to his rescue and made donations. Jesse Lowe, the man who had ridden from Los Angeles to El Monte to deliver the newspaper to Lorenzo, said that he would obtain animals and accompany him to Fort Yuma. They left El Monte bound for the fort, a distance of two hundred and fifty miles, early on the morning of March 10th, 1856.

Lorenzo and Jesse were about ten days in reaching the fort. During that journey, he was haunted by the fear that the rescued girl might not be his sister. But when they finally arrived at the fort, Olive came out to meet him. He was overjoyed to see that it was truly his sister. She was now nineteen, grown to womanhood, but despite the traces of outdoor life, facial tattoos, and barbarous treatment, he knew her at once. Lorenzo was now twenty, a young man. For a long time, they stared at each other, each reliving that horrible scene on the Gila trail, their parents, brothers, and sisters sprawled in their own blood. Then they embraced and wept. For an entire hour, neither of them could speak.

A large gathering of Americans, Indians, and Mexicans witnessed the reunion of Olive and Lorenzo. There was not a dry eye in the crowd. Even the Indians were moved, and more than one raised his hand to brush a tear from his cheek.

When they could finally control their emotions, Olive and Lorenzo talked for hours, avoiding any mention of the massacre. Lorenzo told her about his miraculous survival, how the Kellys and Wilders had found him and brought him to Fort Yuma. He told her of the kindness of Dr. Hewitt and that he had gone to San Francisco with him and his family. They reminisced about their childhood and shared happy memories of their days on the farm in Fulton, Illinois. Those days seemed like a dream now.

When Lorenzo thought Olive was ready to talk about it, he ventured to ask a question: "And what of Mary Ann?"

Olive hesitated, not trusting her emotions to re-live that terrible time. Then she began.

"In 1853, when we had been among the Mojaves for a year, the Colorado River did not overflow its banks, and, without irrigation, the crops failed. There was a great famine, and Mary Ann became very ill, mostly from starvation. I tried to find blackbird eggs and roots to keep her alive, but it was no use. She became weaker and weaker and finally passed away. She died peacefully, and I was allowed to bury her near our little garden plot. The Mojaves wanted to burn her body, which is their tradition, but I begged and pleaded until the chief finally acquiesced and granted my request. Oh, Lorenzo, it was so hard to leave her behind in her little grave among the Indians."

Lorenzo looked at Olive, his eyes welling up with tears.

"What about you, Olive? How were you able to survive, and why did they put marks on your face?"

Olive told him about the kindness of Aespaneo and Topeka and how they had given her their seed corn while their own people were starving to death. Then, she put her hand to her chin.

"It is their custom to tattoo their women when they reach marriageable age. And this brings me to this thing I must tell you, Lorenzo. I hope you will not judge me harshly, as I had little choice in the matter." She looked away and bit her lower lip. Then she turned back to Lorenzo and spoke in low tones, almost a whisper.

"In order to survive, I became the wife of the chief's son. We had two beautiful sons, but I had to leave them behind with their father. I was told that many soldiers would come and kill the entire tribe unless I went to the fort with Francisco." She covered her face with her hands and sobbed uncontrollably.

Lorenzo was shocked. At first, he refused to believe her. He shook his head in denial.

"Oh, no, Olive," he said, "you must not tell anyone about this. People can be so cruel. You will be treated like a common squaw, or worse."

"Oh, Lorenzo, if I could but see my children again, I wouldn't care what people thought."

"Then think of the children. They would be miserable among the whites. They would be taunted and ridiculed. Is that what you want for them?"

"Of course, you are right, Lorenzo, but my heart breaks. I have lost everything I love."

Chapter XXXV
Journey to Oregon

On March 26, 1856, Olive and Lorenzo traveled west with the government train that regularly crossed the desert between Fort Yuma and San Diego to pick up supplies for the fort. They arrived in San Diego at the end of March and promptly departed for the Monte in Los Angeles County, arriving there on April 4th. They went directly to the Willow Brook Inn, where they were welcomed by the proprietors and old friends, the Thompsons. Susan Thompson was now Susan Lewis and was living on a ranch with her husband, David.

Susan embraced Olive, and the two cried together as they remembered Olive's sister, Lucy, who had been Susan's best friend. Susan and her husband insisted she stay with them on the ranch. Soon, the newspapers began to send reporters to interview Olive.

An article appeared in the *Los Angeles Star* stating that Olive had become the wife of the chief's son and had two Indian children. This was the second time they had alluded to Olive's marriage to a Mojave chief.

Due to the strong denial of Lorenzo and others who had known Olive when she traveled west with the Brewsterites, the *Star* printed a retraction saying that Olive had never married and was treated with respect by the Indians. If the *Star* had not retracted the articles, Olive would have been ostracized, as polite society in the 1850s could never accept the fact that a white woman was married to an Indian.

However, many years later, Susan Thompson Lewis Parish would write, "After the famine, Olive became the wife of the chief's son, and, at the time of her rescue, was the mother of two little boys. For four months, Olive lived with us, but she was a grieving, unsatisfied woman who shook one's belief in civilization. We tried to erase the tattoo marks from her face, but we could not erase the wild life from her heart."

While living with the Lewises, Olive and Lorenzo received a letter from an older cousin, Harvey B. Oatman, informing them that he was on his way to El Monte to take them to his home in Phoenix Mills, Oregon Territory, where he farmed and managed a stage station. He arrived at the Monte on June 3, 1856. Ira Thompson was skeptical and insisted on seeing his identification and proof that he was, indeed, related to Olive and Lorenzo. He was able to produce the required credentials, and Ira Thompson reluctantly let Olive and Lorenzo go with him. Before leaving El Monte, Susan gave Olive a slip of paper with Robert's address on it. He had written to the Thompsons telling them about the cattle ranch he and John owned near San Diego. The Thompsons had the impression that Robert had prospered and was still a bachelor.

On June 16, 1856, they departed El Monte for San Pedro, where they boarded a steamer bound for San Francisco. During their stopover in San Francisco, Olive was interviewed by a reporter from the *San Francisco Evening Bulletin* on June 22, 1856. The interview appeared in the *Bulletin* on June 24, 1856.

Alone in her San Francisco hotel room, Olive penned a letter to Robert Kelly. Robert received Olive's letter and kept it for the rest of his life. It read as follows:

> I feel once more like myself since I have risen from the dead and landed once more in a sivalized world. The events of the past five years of my life has been misery and dispare. I have ben a slave to those fiends that committed the bloody masicre, to toile and work for them that had the blood of them that were near and dear to me stained up under thare hands that driven the happy smiles from my brow and be diewed my life with tears. It seems like a dream to me to look back and see what I had ben thrue and just now waking up.

This letter, written just four months after her arrival at Fort Yuma, is indicative of Olive's struggle with the English language after five years of disuse. Olive included her address in Oregon territory, but she would never receive a reply. When Robert died in 1890, Olive's letter was still among his possessions.

The day after their arrival in San Francisco, Olive, Lorenzo, and cousin Harvey boarded a boat in San Francisco Bay and steamed up the Sacramento River to Red Bluff. From there, they traveled by stagecoach over the Siskiyou Mountains to the Rogue River Valley of Oregon.

Upon their arrival, Olive and Lorenzo marveled at the lush green of the valley and the tall, dense conifer forests that covered the mountainside.

Olive remarked, "Oh, what a difference this is from the harsh, dry desert where I have lived the past five years."

The first settlers of this region were miners in search of gold and silver in the mountains bordering the Rogue River and Bear Creek. This was only about three years before Olive and Lorenzo arrived, but more whites had settled here since and had carved out several small towns and farms. Other accoutrements of civilization arrived with mills to process wheat and timber. In 1851, there were an estimated ninety-five hundred Indians in Rogue River country, but bitter clashes between whites and Indians brought on a "war of extermination" in the fall of 1855. By the time the war ended in June1856, as many as seven thousand Indians had been killed. The survivors were forced into a reservation on the Oregon coast.

Chapter XXXVI
The Book

While living in Oregon Territory, Lorenzo and Olive worked on their cousin's farm and helped out at the Oatman Hotel, which was owned by Harvey's brother, Harrison, or Harry, as he preferred to be called. Olive became friendly with Abigail Taylor and her daughter, Rachel. She went to live with the Taylor family for a while, and Abigail taught her to sew. Rachel was a teacher who taught Olive to read and write. A granddaughter of Abigail Taylor wrote:

> Olive sometimes paced the floor for hours, weeping. We often heard her pacing the floor all night. She seemed ashamed of the tattoo marks etched deeply into her chin. She would cover them with her hand when she met anyone.

While in Oregon, Olive and Lorenzo met the Reverend Royal B. Stratton, a young, well-educated minister. He was pastor of a Methodist church in Yreka, California, but made frequent trips to the Rogue River area to preach to Methodists and perform baptisms, weddings, and other ministerial functions. He was interested in Olive's and Lorenzo's story and offered to write a book based on their experiences. Harvey Oatman encouraged Lorenzo to have a book published to counteract "inaccurate press coverage." Lorenzo and Olive agreed. They hoped that the book would be a success and that some of the proceeds would help pay for their education. Lorenzo borrowed the money to cover the cost of publication.

The Reverend Stratton commenced work on the book at once. The title was *The Captivity of the Oatman Girls,* and it was published in San Francisco in 1857.

The book caused a sensation and quickly sold out. So great was the demand that a second edition was soon printed. Olive and Lorenzo returned to California to attend the University of the Pacific in Santa Clara for the 1857-58 school year.

However, after a few months at school, they were contacted by the Reverend Stratton. He was engaged in negotiations with a New York publisher to print a third edition. He proposed that Olive and Lorenzo come with him to Albany, New York, where they could stay at his home with him, his wife, and their young son, Albert, while giving lectures to promote book sales.

Olive and Lorenzo traveled to San Francisco with the Stratton family, where they boarded the steamship *Golden Age,* bound for Panama on March 5, 1858. Twelve days later, they arrived in Panama, where they took a ferry to the Panama railroad terminal. There, they boarded an open-sided train and traveled forty-seven miles across the Isthmus of Panama to Aspinwall, where they boarded a steamer bound for New York. The entire journey took twenty-one days.

When they had settled in at the Stratton home in Albany, Olive and Lorenzo visited their mother's relatives, the Sperry family, in Rochester, New York. It was a time of smiles mingled with tears—smiles to be among family they had never met and tears as they remembered their mother, Mary Ann Sperry Oatman, a sweet, loving woman who met with a violent end.

On May 15, 1858, the third edition of their book was released. Olive and Lorenzo resumed their education in the Albany schools while the Reverend Stratton feverishly made arrangements with various churches throughout the state of New York for them to speak. He received many enthusiastic responses to his proposals, especially since he had promised the pastors a percentage of the admission fees. He set up a lecture tour and sent posters to the churches so they could advertise the event.

The Reverend Stratton exhibited flair for showmanship when he had Olive photographed wearing a stylish, floor-length, bouffant dress of an expensive silk fabric with a demure lace collar. The stroke of genius was the soutache braid trim around the hem, cuffs, and upper sleeves of the garment in a pattern which resembled the tattoos on her chin. The effect was startling. Wherever these posters appeared, they aroused so much curiosity that people flocked to see her.

The lecture halls were always filled. Lorenzo played a supporting role at these events, filling in some of the details of his survival and unrelenting determination to find his sisters. Olive's lecture notes have been preserved and can be read today.

Chapter XXXVII
Stratton Drops Lorenzo

In June of 1858, Lorenzo and Olive traveled to Whiteside County, Illinois, to visit Asa and Sarah Abbott. Sarah was their mother's sister, and Olive and Lorenzo had seen them frequently when they were growing up in Fulton. Their mother had corresponded with the Abbotts on the westward journey. Whenever they stopped near a fort or a stage stop, their mother would post a letter to her sister.

It was a happy but tearful reunion. Mr. Abbott had written to Major Heintzelman at Fort Yuma as soon as he had learned about the massacre, asking for details of the event and what Heintzelman was doing to obtain the release of Olive and Mary Ann. He had received a response from Heintzelman with details of the massacre, as he understood it, but any reference to rescue efforts were vague and non-committal.

There was plenty of work to be done on the Abbott farm, and Olive and Lorenzo pitched in to help. Lorenzo helped his uncle with the animals and the crops, while Olive performed many of the household chores to lighten her aunt's burden.

They had been at the Abbott farm for about a month when a letter arrived from the Reverend Stratton. The book sales were going very well, and he wanted Olive to return to resume her lectures. However, Reverend Stratton made it clear that Lorenzo's services on the lecture circuit were no longer required.

It was with great reluctance that Olive left for New York on January 18, 1859, leaving Lorenzo behind on the Abbott farm. Lorenzo continued to help with the farm work, and, in June of 1860, met Edna Amelia Canfield, the girl next door, who became his wife on August 2, 1860.

For a while, Lorenzo and Edna lived in Whiteside County, Illinois, and later moved to Minnesota before settling in Red Cloud, Nebraska, where they built and ran a hotel for several years. His obituary in the

Red Cloud Chief on October 11, 1901, states that Lorenzo Oatman was born near Fulton, Illinois, on July 13, 1836, and died at age sixty-five. He was buried at the Red Cloud Cemetery.

(IRETABA, CAIROOK and CAIROOK'S SECOND WIFE WITH CHILD)

Painting by Balduin Möllhausen with the Ives Expedition, 1857-1858

Chapter XXXVIII
The Ives Expedition

A year or so after Olive's release, the Mojaves and the Yumas went to war against their old enemies, the Cocopahs. This time, the outcome was different. The Cocopahs triumphed, and many Mojaves were killed. When Olive learned of this, she was glad she had left, as she might have been killed in retaliation for the death of the Mojave warriors. Her status had been elevated when she married Cairook, but she was still a *Hicco* (white), and any misfortune the tribe might suffer would be attributed to her. She doubted that even Cairook could have protected her against the bloodthirsty savages once their need for vengeance was aroused.

In 1857-1858, Lt. Joseph C. Ives was chosen to conduct a second survey of the thirty-fifth parallel for the Central Pacific Railway. This time, he was to travel by boat up the Colorado River. He had been a member of the Whipple survey team four years before and was familiar with the Indians of the area. He contacted Balduin Müllhausen, suggesting that he accompany the expedition to sketch landmarks and the indigenous peoples along the route. His sketches are included in Lt. Ives' journal entitled *Report Upon the Colorado River of the West,* published in 1861.

The most pertinent of these drawings was a portrait of Iretaba (Yara Tav), Cairook, and an unidentified female holding an infant. It is presumed that the female is Cairook's second wife, as the drawing is purported to have been completed in 1858, two years after Olive left the tribe.

In his journal, Ives states:

The Mojaves have noble figures, and the stature of some is gigantic. The men wear no clothing but a strip of cotton cloth. Most have intelligent countenances and agreeable expressions. Women over the age of twenty are almost invariably short and stout with fat, good-natured faces.

Women have only one article of dress—a short petticoat made of strips of bark sticking out about eight inches behind. Some of the younger girls are very pretty and have slender, graceful figures. The children are naked and have a precocious, impish look.

Sub-chiefs wear a white feather tipped with crimson. This rank is, to some extent, hereditary. We traded beads for beans, corn, wheat, and pumpkins. They also raise watermelons but these were not yet in season.

Lt. Whipple passed through this valley in 1854. One of the five sub-chiefs, Cairook, and Iretaba (Yara Tav), the younger brother of Chief Espaniole, joined him as guides and accompanied him through the country west of the Colorado as far as the Mormon Road that leads to Los Angeles. They are noble specimens of their race and rendered the party invaluable service. I have been inquiring after them with the hope of meeting them again and have learned that Cairook still lives and retains his authority.

The name of Iretaba the Indians do not recognize, and it is possible some mistake was made about his appellation. (Ives was correct in this assumption, as his Mojave name is Yara Tav.)

The Mojaves favor the color red for cloth or blankets. They highly prize small, white beads, but will not accept blue and red beads as a gift, except for large, blue glass beads, which they intersperse with the white in their necklaces.

Twenty-four men in an open boat, half the time stuck on a bar, could be greatly harassed by six or seven hundred Indians concealed in the thickets that line the river.

One morning, I glanced up to see my old friend, Iretaba, standing on a dock close by. He was delighted at being recognized and told me that his chief, Cairook, lived across the river and would soon come to see me. I asked Iretaba to accompany us on the boat, and, upon arrival of the pack train, to go eastward with us. He expressed his willingness to do so. I gave him some blankets and other articles. When he and Cairook parted from Lt. Whipple, they were loaded with enough presents to make them rich. However, it is their custom to burn their possessions when a relative dies and to whose memory they wish to pay special tribute.

The appearance of a great crowd on the opposite bank indicated the presence of Cairook, and, in a few minutes, a messenger swam out to the boat and asked me to send a boat over. This was impossible to do, and I sent word that he must furnish his own transportation. A raft was provided, and four of his tribe, one at each corner, propelled him over. He stood erect in the middle of the raft, and the water was alive with his swimming followers.

Cairook is a noble-looking man. He is nearly six and a half foot tall, has a magnificent figure and a fine, open face. He seemed glad to see me and laughed a great deal as he alluded to former adventures. He inquired about Lt. Whipple, for whom he had an exalted opinion. Cairook spent the whole day with me. I gave him plenty to eat and some tobacco.

For two days, Cairook, at my invitation, traveled upon the steamboat. He was accompanied the first day by his wife. She was a nice-looking squaw, and I allowed her and her spouse the privilege of sitting upon the upper deck. They sat in dignified state, enjoying the admiring gaze of their neighbors. From the airs that were put on by Madam Cairook, I'm afraid the trip turned her head.

As we steamed away from the Mojave villages, we passed a conspicuous, conical peak a few miles east of the river which stands almost upon the thirty-fifth parallel opposite the initial point of the California boundary. Cairook bade us goodbye and returned home. Iretaba is to remain. He has brought along a lad of sixteen by the name of Nah-va-rup-pa to keep him company. Since the meeting with Cairook, our relations with the Mojaves has been quite favorable. They have, at every stopping point, brought provisions to trade.

Chapter XXXIX
Death of Cairook

In August of 1858, the Rose-Baley wagon train was attacked by Mojaves near the Colorado River on the newly surveyed Beale Wagon Road, now known as Route 66. An eyewitness account, written by L.J. Rose, was published on November 29, 1859, one year later, by the Missouri Republican

According to Rose, his wagon train had set up camp near the Colorado River on August 27, 1858. They drove their livestock to the river to drink. The men from the Baley wagon train, which was camped on the edge of the Mojave Valley, also drove their cattle to the river to drink, intending to return to their camp later.

They had seen Mojaves but they had been friendly. When the Rose party moved to the riverbank on August 29th, they were visited by two Mojave sub-chiefs and their retinues. They were Cairook and Sikahot. Rose states that gifts were exchanged. The chiefs asked if they were planning to settle here, but the emigrants replied that they intended to move on to California.

On August 30th, the Rose party moved their camp a mile down the river from "Beale's Crossing". They turned their livestock loose to graze. Suddenly, about 250 Indians appeared. They surrounded the camp and began to discharge arrows. The Rose party opened fire, killing seventeen Mojaves, one of whom was a sub-chief. More Indians appeared, and proceeded to drive off the cattle and horses. Of the twenty-five men in the Rose party, one was killed and eleven were wounded. .The emigrants panicked and headed back the way they had come.

Rose said the emigrants had lost all but seventeen of their four hundred head of cattle, and all but ten of their thirty-seven horses. They retained two mules, but lost all of their equipment and supplies. As they headed back to Albuquerque, 560 miles away, they met the

Baley party and two other wagon trains heading west. All turned back sharing whatever supplies they had. When the survivors finally reached Albuquerque, they were destitute and starving. .

According to a Mojave known as Jo Nelson (Chooksa Homar), in an interview with anthropologist A.L. Kroeber in 1903, there was no exchange of gifts, as stated by Rose. Nelson told Kroeber, through an interpreter, that the emigrants had entered Mojave territory without asking permission, turned their livestock out to graze on Mojave crops, and cut down cottonwood trees to make rafts for crossing the river. He explained that cottonwoods were very valuable to the Mojave. They provided shade from the hot sun, lumber for house poles and fabric for clothing. (The soft, inner bark was used for women's skirts). The Mojaves had been told that white men intended to enslave them and take their wives and children. Five sub-chiefs recruited many warriors, including a large number of Chemehuevi's, to defend their territory against the white invaders.

When L.J. Rose's account appeared in the Missouri Republican a year after the attack on the Rose-Baley wagon train, General N.S. Clarke, commander of the Military Department in San Francisco, sent Lieutenant Colonel William Hoffman to the Colorado River to establish a military post at "Beale's Crossing" to protect emigrants passing through Troops were to follow.

When Hoffman and his troops reached Beaver Lake, they had a minor skirmish with Mojaves. No one was killed. General Clarke interpreted it as a "hostile act." He ordered Hoffman to march against the Mojaves and Chemehuevis. Seven- hundred troops were allocated for this purpose. When all of the troops were assembled at Beale's crossing, Hoffman was able to establish a post with no resistance from the Mojaves.

On April 23, 1859, Hoffman marched his seven-hundred troops into the village and demanded that the Great Chief, Espaniole, sign a peace treaty with the U.S. Government which would give emigrants the right to cross Mojave lands unmolested. He threatened to lay waste to the

Mojave crops if his demands were not met, and the Mojaves would not be permitted to plant again.

In addition, Hoffman demanded hostages to ensure the peace was kept and no further attacks on emigrants would occur. He took two sons of sub-chiefs, four brothers of sub-chiefs and two nephews of sub-chiefs. Lastly, he took the sub-chief who led the attack on him and his men at Beaver Lake, the same chief identified by Mr. Rose as one of those responsible for the attack on his wagon train – Cairook.

Espaniole was devastated. His only son would be imprisoned. He pleaded with Hoffman.

"We will punish the guilty ones," he said.

Hoffman shook his head. "No, it is not acceptable. However, at the end of a year, if there are no further attacks on emigrants, the hostages will be released."

Espaniole was inconsolable. He could not imagine Cairook, who had always been brave and free, locked up in a tiny cell. His tears coursed down his wrinkled old face as he bid goodbye to his beloved son. He felt as if his heart were torn from his chest. To Cairook, he looked very old and frail with defeat written on every aspect of his being.

As soon as the treaty was signed, Colonel Hoffman dispatched Major Armistead, two companies of infantry, and a detachment of artillery to secure Beale's crossing. Here, they would begin construction of a fort. It would later be called Fort Mojave.

On April 24, 1859, Cairook and the other hostages departed for Fort Yuma with the soldiers. Not a shot had been fired. The tribe had been spared.

The nine hostages found incarceration at Fort Yuma intolerable and, in late June of 1860, when they had not been released after one year, as promised, they plotted their escape. They had nearly suffocated in the cramped cell in 120-degree heat during the summer months and came close to freezing to death in the winter. On a particularly hot day, one of Cairook's cousins had begged a guard to slit his throat. They were unwilling to go through another summer. Cairook told the others of his plan. The next day when they were let out of their cells for fresh air, Cairook seized and held the guard as the others ran for the river. Cairook was bayoneted in the stomach and shot. One other hostage was caught and killed, but the others escaped by diving into the river and swimming underwater until they were out of the range of rifle fire.

Chapter XXXX
Olive Learns of Cairook's Death

In February of 1864, Olive heard that a delegation of Mojaves, accompanied by a Captain John Moss, had journeyed to the East Coast to meet with President Lincoln on matters relating to the tribe and their lands. "Captain" Moss, somewhat of a confidence man and adventurer, had become acquainted with the Mojave tribe when he traveled west in search of gold. He became a friend, interpreter, and guide to the Mojave and hoped to be appointed as a government agent for the tribe.

Olive learned that the chief was a member of the Mojave delegation and that they were currently ensconced in the fashionable Metropolitan Hotel on Broadway in New York City. She hoped to arrange a meeting with the chief, though she was uncertain whether it would be the old chief, Espaniole, or Cairook. The old chief had been showing signs of decline before she left the tribe, and, even if he were still alive, she doubted that he would be physically able to make the journey across the country. She was certain that Cairook had succeeded him as great chief of the Mojave.

It was with great trepidation that Olive boarded the train for New York City. What if Cairook refused to see her? She decided that she had nothing to lose. She intended to ask him about their two children. She had never stopped thinking about them and hoped it might be possible to see them again someday. Perhaps she would ask Cairook to take her with him.

She had become weary of the lecture circuit, and the only times she was somewhat content were the hours she spent in the classroom or studying at home. By now, she was resigned to being a spinster for the rest of her life. She could not conceive of any white man wanting her for a wife with the marks of her captivity indelibly tattooed upon her face.

When she arrived in New York City, she went directly to the Metropolitan Hotel. She walked briskly toward the reception desk with a show of confidence she did not feel.

"I wish to see Captain John Moss, if he is available, please," she said.

"Captain Moss is presently in the reception room with the visiting Mojave delegation. Whom shall I say is calling?"

Olive replied, "Olive Oatman."

The receptionist paused, examining her closely, but Olive was wearing a hat with a veil which concealed her face.

A bellhop was dispatched to inform Captain Moss of his visitor. In a few minutes, he returned, followed by a smiling Captain Moss. He was a very handsome man with thick, curly, dark hair, a small mustache, and a small, neatly trimmed beard.

"Miss Oatman, what an honor to meet you. What brings you here to the big city?"

"I wish to see the chief of the Mojaves. As you know, I lived among the Mojaves for five years and consider several of them my friends. When I heard the chief was here, I came down from Albany on the train. I have just arrived."

"I'm sure the chief will be pleased to see you. Come, I'll take you to him."

He took Olive's arm, and together they walked toward the reception room.

When they entered the spacious, high-ceilinged room, Olive was struck with the grandeur of the place. There were huge windows draped in red velvet, paneled walls with gold moldings, fine Persian carpets, and chairs upholstered in red damask. A massive crystal chandelier hung from the ceiling in the center of the room, while fresh flowers graced the piano and the polished mahogany tables placed about the room for the convenience of the guests. She could not help but contrast this opulence with the humble hogans of the Mojave village.

She hesitated at the door, her heart pounding. Would Cairook be pleased to see her, or would he have her expelled from the reception room? Captain Moss took her over to where the chief sat surrounded by reporters. She maneuvered her way through the ring of newsmen, and when she came face to face with the chief, she was shocked and disappointed.

It was not Cairook, nor was it the old chief, Espaniole. It was Yara Tav, the old chief's younger brother. She was speechless. As soon as she regained her composure, she approached Yara Tav and lifted the veil on her hat. He recognized her at once by the *ki-i-chook* on her chin. He stopped talking to the reporters and stared at her in disbelief.

Olive greeted him in the Mojave language. He dismissed the reporters and motioned to Captain Moss to bring a chair for Olive. For a while, they exchanged pleasantries until she could no longer contain her curiosity.

"How did you become chief? What of Espaniole and Cairook?" she asked.

Yara Tav related the story of the "attack" by seven hundred soldiers and the taking of Cairook and eight others to Fort Yuma as hostages. He told her that the white soldiers had promised to release them in a year, but that promise was not kept. Cairook and the other hostages decided to escape. He told her about Cairook's bravery and how he had saved the lives of his cousins but lost his own.

Olive felt as if the air had been sucked from her lungs. Her heart seemed to leap from her chest. She could not accept the fact that Cairook was dead. She shook her head in denial. "No, this cannot be," she said, her voice breaking as she fought the tears that clouded her eyes. She had always thought of Cairook as being strong and immortal. Now, the tears ran freely down her face. She took a handkerchief from her bag and dabbed at her eyes.

Yara Tav continued, "After Cairook's death at Fort Yuma, my brother, Espaniole, became very sick and was unable to carry out his duties as chief. A council meeting was held, and I was elected to succeed him as great chief until his grandson, your son, Empote-John, is old enough to become great chief."

"And what of my two sons? Now they are without mother or father. Who is caring for them?" she asked anxiously. She gripped the arms of her chair, bracing herself against possible bad news.

Yara Tav smiled.

"They are fine, healthy boys, tall and strong like their father."

She exhaled, relief and joy flooding through her.

"Who is caring for them?" she asked.

"Aespaneo and Tokwa Oa. Tokwa Oa is married now. Your sons are as her own. She often speaks of you and hopes you will return when you tire of life among the whites."

Olive smiled as she thought of Topeka. It was comforting to know that her dear friend was caring for her sons. They would want for nothing.

Yara Tav told her that the Mojaves now had the desire to become civilized. Olive imparted her best wishes to Topeka, Aespaneo, and her other Mojave friends.

Satisfied that her children were in good hands, she said her goodbyes, shaking hands with the left hand in the Mojave tradition. She took her leave, experiencing a heaviness of heart that she thought she had conquered over the past eight years.

As she rode home on the train, she tried to imagine what her boys would look like today. She prayed they would possess their father's strength of character and his kindness. If Yara Tav had spoken the truth about the tribe's willingness to become "civilized," perhaps they would abandon their barbarous customs. The killing and the torture would end. She prayed it would be so, for her children's sake.

She stared out the window at the darkened landscape where a long-repressed memory took form. She envisioned Cairook as he emerged from the river that day, tall and victorious, the droplets of water clinging to his dark skin. She was overwhelmed by a sense of loss so profound that a tremor shook her entire body. She reached for her handkerchief as the tears coursed down her cheeks. Averting her face to avoid the stares of other passengers, her trembling hand moved beneath the heavy veil, wiping the tears from her eyes.

The next morning, the local newspaper carried a photograph of the Mojave delegation, accompanied by an interview with the chief. It said,

When asked by a reporter what he thought of the Americans, Yara Tav replied, "Yara Tav heap see 'em *'Mericanos. 'Mericanos* too much talk, too much eat, too much drink; no work, no raise pumpkins, corn, watermelons. All time walk, talk, drink ... no good!"

One thing that Yara Tav neglected to tell Olive was that Cairook had taken another wife soon after Olive left the Mojaves.

JOHN BRANT FAIRCHILD

Chapter XXXXI
John Fairchild

Olive continued to lecture until she met Major John Brant Fairchild.

John Fairchild had almost lost his life in 1854 while driving a herd of Texas longhorns through New Mexico Territory with his two brothers. They were riding through the Santa Cruz Mountains of Sonora, Mexico, when Apaches attacked them, scattering the hired hands. Before the drivers could fire, the Indians had sacked the wagons and run off two hundred head of cattle, leaving John's brother, Dr. B. Homer Fairchild, dead.

He had been a successful cattleman for many years, but now, at the age of thirty-five, John Fairchild was ready for a change. He was now inclined to utilize his considerable business acumen to open his own bank. He knew it would take a great deal of capital, so he began to seek investors. At the same time, he sought to acquire experience by working with various bankers in an effort to learn all he could about the business. One of these bankers was an old friend, Henry Morgan of Albany, New York.

It was a lovely spring day when the two men decided to walk to Henry's office from the hotel where John was staying and where they had just enjoyed a hearty breakfast. They were passing an elementary school when John noticed an attractive young woman walking toward the school building in the company of a large group of children. At first, he assumed she was a teacher, but then the teacher appeared and ordered the children to line up. When they had done so, she led them into the building. He turned to his friend.

"Henry, look at that group of children. There's a young woman among them who appears to be one of the students."

"That's exactly what she is, John. That's Olive Oatman. You may have heard of her. The Oatman family was attacked by Indians on the

Gila Trail in 1851. There were nine of them, but only three survived the massacre. She and her little sister were taken captive by the Apaches and later traded to the Mojaves. Her sister died a year later. One brother survived the attack, but was badly beaten. He was found by two families that were part of the original wagon train the Oatmans had been traveling west with. He was taken to Fort Yuma, where he received medical treatment. Olive was ransomed from the Mojaves in 1856. The Mojaves tattooed her chin. It isn't noticeable from this distance, but closer up, it's disfiguring. It's a shame, because she is otherwise a very attractive woman."

"I'd like to meet her."

"I think that can be arranged. She's lecturing at the Methodist Church tonight. My wife and I plan to attend. I'm a member of the church. I'll ask Reverend Wilson to introduce you. The lecture starts at 7:00. We'll pick you up at 6:30."

"I'll be ready."

John and Olive were introduced that evening, and John began to court her. She was staying with her uncle, Moses Sperry, and his wife, Milly, in Rochester at the time. John became a frequent visitor to their home. He was thirty-five years old, quite distinguished-looking, with a full, dark beard and dark brown hair with touches of grey at the temples. Olive was somewhat surprised by his attentions. She was twenty-eight years old and had accepted the fact that she would never marry. She couldn't imagine that any man would find her attractive. However, John apparently did. He seemed not to notice her tattoos, or, if he did, he seemed not to care. Olive's aunt was as surprised by John's interest in Olive as Olive was. One morning, when they were alone, Aunt Milly said, "Olive, you are a very fortunate young woman. John Fairchlld is obviously a man of means and very capable of supporting you. But, more importantly, he appears to be a man of character who puts substance before beauty."

Olive and John were married in Rochester, New York, on November 9, 1865.

The newlyweds moved to Farmington, Michigan, about twenty miles west of Detroit, where John had been raised and where his three sisters still lived. John purchased a farm with the money he had earned driving cattle from Mexico to California, where cattle brought high prices. John led his last cattle drive in the spring of 1866. He bought a herd of Mexican longhorns in Texas and drove them north through Arkansas to Missouri, where they were loaded on rail cars bound for Chicago. They lived in Farmington for five years before moving to Niles City, Michigan, where John became involved in money brokerage.

Chapter XXXXII
The Bonfire

One evening, while Olive and John were still living in Farmington, Olive sat in her upstairs bedroom, reading by lamplight. She thought she smelled smoke and ran to the window. Looking down at the garden below, she was surprised to see John Fairchild feeding the flames of a huge bonfire. As she watched, he picked up two objects and hurled them into the blaze. His face, in the glow of the flames, was contorted in rage. Olive withdrew from the window and walked slowly toward the bed. She lifted the coverlet and slid in. Then she reached up and extinguished the lamp. She said her prayers and lay there in the darkness, watching the reflection of the flames flicker across the ceiling. She shivered despite the warmth of the night. At last, she fell into a restless sleep.

Hours later, John approached the bedroom door, and, seeing that Olive was asleep, chose not to disturb her. He walked quickly and quietly down the hall to another bedroom.

The next morning, Olive awoke early, dressed hurriedly, and crept downstairs to the main floor. She walked through the house and out the back door.

"Going somewhere?" The voice seemed to come from nowhere.

She stood still, her heart pounding.

"You're up early, my dear." It was John's voice.

She turned and looked up at the porch where John stood leaning against the doorjamb.

"I wanted to see what you were burning last night," she answered truthfully.

"Well, why didn't you just ask me?" he replied, walking down the steps toward her.

She continued to look at him, not daring to speak.

"I'll tell you what I was burning. I've been collecting every damn copy of Stratton's book I could get my hands on. They're all there in the burn pile, what's left of them."

"But why. John?"

"Because there isn't an ounce of truth in them. He writes this fanciful tale of the virgin captive among savages. It sells like hotcakes. Then he drags you around the country and puts you on exhibition like some carnival freak. The pious Reverend Stratton exploited you, my dear. And where is all the money he made on you, all those book royalties and admission fees he charged people to see you? He was supposed to pay for your education, but he didn't come through, did he?" John was livid now.

"I had a few months schooling in Santa Clara, and when I met you, I was attending school in Albany," she replied.

"Public school. Didn't cost him a penny. He's a self-righteous, pompous ass, and his book is a pack of lies."

"What do you mean, John?" she asked, disingenuously.

"You know exactly what I mean, Olive. The rumors persist that you were married to the son of the Mojave chief and bore two sons and that you had to leave them behind when you were ransomed. Your old friend, Susan Thompson, told an interviewer that when you stayed with her and her husband at the Monte, you were very distraught and cried for the loss of your two children."

Olive's face blanched white. She covered her face with her hands and walked quickly toward the house. She dropped her hands to her sides, held her head erect, and squared her shoulders. She walked toward the porch steps and began to climb them.

John shouted after her. "And what happened when you were with the Apaches? They are a filthy, rapacious lot. It's hard to imagine that any young girl could live among them for a year and remain pure."

At the top step, she halted as if struck by a bullet to her back. She wheeled about to face John. Tears filled her eyes and cascaded down her face.

"Are you quite through with me, John?" Her voice was barely audible.

She turned and walked through the open door. She ascended the long staircase and entered her room. Once inside, she locked the door behind her and flung herself across the bed. She cried into her pillow for almost an hour and then fell into an exhausted sleep. She slept until noon. When she arose, she went to the washstand and poured water from the pitcher into the bowl. She washed and dried her face and went downstairs.

John had left for his office at the bank, and she had the house to herself. She made tea in the kitchen and sat at the kitchen table, drinking her tea and eating biscuits and jam. She was relieved to be alone.

That evening, when John returned, Olive was in the kitchen, preparing dinner. He walked over and put his arms around her.

"Olive, my dear, I'm so sorry. I don't know what possessed me. I love you, and I understand. You had no control over your situation. You did what you had to do to survive. None of it was your fault, and I had no right suggest it was. Can you forgive me?

"Yes, John," she muttered, still pained by his earlier accusations.

"I love you very much, and I promise I will never mention the past again. Please forgive me."

She turned and faced him. She saw the love in his eyes and heard the sincerity in his voice.

"You are forgiven. Perhaps we can start over and put the past behind us." She kissed his cheek and turned back to her cooking.

After dinner, Olive turned to John.

"John, it's time for me to be honest with you. You deserve to know the truth, and I'm not going to sugar-coat it. I should have told you at the start and we could have avoided all this heartbreak. Let's sit down in the parlor and talk. I've made some lemonade."

Olive opened the icebox and took out a pitcher and two cold glasses. She filled the two glasses and returned the pitcher to the icebox. She handed one to John, and together they walked into the parlor and sat down opposite each other.

Olive took a sip of her lemonade and reached to set it down on the little table next to her chair. Her hand trembled, and she nearly spilled her drink. She took a deep breath.

"I'll begin by telling you about my miserable existence with the Tonto Apaches. After the massacre of my family, Mary Ann and I were driven like dogs for three hundred miles until we reached their squalid little village. During that horrendous journey, we were beaten unmercifully if we fell behind, but I was not violated. When we arrived at the village, we were turned over to the chief to be disposed of as he saw fit. I later learned that our captors had told the chief we were virgins and therefore more valuable. They hoped to curry favor with him, as he had more horses and other desirable goods than any other member of the tribe. Fortunately for me, he was impotent, although he never gave up trying. I had to look out for the other men, though. I tried to stay close to the chief's house, but sometimes I had to fetch water at a spring at the edge of the village. A few times, I was followed and caught. I would threaten to tell the chief, and sometimes it worked, and sometimes it didn't. On those occasions that it didn't, I would cope by blocking out what was happening to my body and praying for my immortal soul.

"The old chief had two old wives that ordered us about and beat us if we were not quick enough. We were also slaves to everyone else, including the children. If not for Mary Ann, I would have killed myself. After a year of interminable hell, Topeka arrived at the village. She saw how cruelly we were treated, and when she returned to her home with the Mojaves, she begged her father, Chief Espaniole, to buy us from the Apaches. At first, he resisted. She told him we would be her "little sisters." The old chief relented and gave her blankets, vegetables, and a horse to trade for us.

"She and two Mojave braves returned and bought us. We traveled about three hundred miles to their village on the Colorado River. It was spring, the cottonwoods were leafing out, and the grass was fresh and green. Mary Ann was thrilled.

"We lived in the chief's house with his wife, Aespaneo, and Topeka. We were given a small plot of earth and some seeds to plant. But we were still slaves and had to fetch firewood and gather mesquite berries for the family of the chief and any others who wished to order us about.

"Topeka and Aespaneo saw to it that I was not molested by the male tribal members. During our captivity with the Apaches and the Mojaves, Mary Ann was never in danger of sexual assault: she was too young.

"Then the drought struck in 1853, and Mary Ann died of starvation. I myself was on the brink of starvation, but Aespaneo saved me by giving me a gruel made from seed corn that she had hidden while people were dying of starvation all around us.

"The river overflowed in early 1854 and irrigated the fields. We had a great harvest that fall, and the danger of starvation was past. Then the Mojaves went to war against the Cocopahs, and the Mojaves won. They did not lose a single warrior. If they had, I, as a captive, would have been killed as a sacrifice to his spirit. As it was, they brought several Cocopah captives with them. One was a beautiful young woman, but she tried to escape and was brought back and crucified. She was tortured until she died. It was horrible. They forced me and the other captives to watch as a warning against any attempt to escape.

"That night, I was told that the chief's son, Cairook, wanted me for his wife. I had been teaching him English, so I knew him. After what I had just witnessed, I didn't object. There was no hope of escape, so I resigned myself to remaining with the Mojaves, and I felt I would enjoy some protection as the wife of a sub-chief."

Up to this point, Olive's voice was flat and devoid of expression as she recited the litany of her life as a captive. However, her demeanor changed markedly when she spoke of her children. She became animated and choked with emotion.

"Cairook was good to me, and we had two sons. My baby was only two months old when I was ransomed out." Her voice broke, and tears slid down her cheeks. She began to tremble, and soon her body was wracked by sobs.

John, who had remained silent the entire time, suddenly stood up and knelt at her feet. He reached out and enfolded her in his arms.

"Oh, my dear," he said.

When she had regained her composure, she continued.

"Of course, they wouldn't let me take my children. The eldest, Empote, will be Great Chief some day. When I was reunited with Lorenzo, we agreed that it would be unwise to divulge the fact that I had been the wife of an Indian and had two children by him. I would have become an outcast in white society."

"That was probably wise."

"There's more, John. In 1864, the year before I met you, I heard there was a delegation of Mojaves that had come east to see President Lincoln in hopes of retaining their tribal lands. The newspaper said they were currently staying at the Metropolitan Hotel in New York City and that the chief was among them. I took the train down and went to the hotel with the intention of seeing Cairook again, as I was certain that the old chief was dead by then. It had been eight years since I left the tribe. To my surprise, it was not Cairook, but his uncle, Yara Tav, who was now chief. I spoke to him in Mojave and asked why he, and not Cairook, was chief. Then he told me that Cairook had been killed at the Fort Yuma prison in 1860. I was shocked and immediately asked about my two sons. He said they were fine and were being cared for by Topeka and Aespaneo. I was much relieved to hear that.

"On my way home on the train, I wept. I was so disappointed that I did not see Cairook to ask him about our boys. I had even fantasized about returning to the Mojave with Cairook just so I could see them again. I don't think they would have known me after eight years, but I would have been content just to be with them again, if only for a little while."

She suddenly felt very tired, but it was a great relief to have everything out in the open. She looked at John.

"Well, there you have it, John, my whole, sordid past. You can either accept it or, if you can't, I understand. I am prepared to leave. I am not without means, you know. The Reverend Stratton gave me a small allowance so that I could pay my aunt and uncle for my room and board in Rochester. My aunt refused to take the money. She told me to 'save it for a rainy day.' I'm sure she thought I was doomed to spinsterhood because of my tattoo and my questionable past.

"I have relatives in Illinois, Oregon, and Rochester. Then there is Lorenzo and his wife. They would all welcome me. I plan to hire an attorney to secure a share of the book royalties. I would also prevail upon the Reverend Stratton to honor his commitment and pay for my education, as promised. I have always wanted to be a teacher."

"Well, Olive, I see you have given this a good deal of thought. However, I don't want you to go. This is your home. I love you and promise that I will never mention the past again." True to his word, he never did.

Chapter XXXXIII
Her Later Life

Olive and John moved to Sherman, Texas in 1872. This move was prompted by the fact that Sherman had become the junction for thirteen stage lines. John thought it was the perfect town for a new bank.

After moving to Sherman, John founded the City Bank of Sherman. He was active in the Commercial National Bank and had a financial interest in the Grenier-Kelly Company of Dallas, Texas. Olive, with the help of servants, kept their beautiful two-story Victorian home on the corner of fashionable Travis and Moore Streets. She participated in various charities, but was mostly involved in children's causes. She took a particular interest in raising funds for orphans

However, it had become apparent that Olive was unhappy. In November of 1875, John wrote to his sister, Livinia, in Farmington, Michigan.

> Dear Livinia,
> I am writing to you in hopes that you, as a woman, can help me understand Olive's recent behavior. She has never been a very happy woman but of late, she seems to be slipping into a deep melancholia that I am at a loss to comprehend and deal with. I have tried to talk to her about it but any attempt to broach the subject meets with either tears or a stony silence. At times, she will remain in her room for hours. She has moved her personal belongings into one of the spare bedrooms and sleeps there, having left our bed six months ago. Our doctor has examined her but finds no physical cause for her problem.
> Is this common in woman of her age (38)? I am hoping you can provide some insight and advise. Thank you.

Your brother, John

A few weeks later, John received a response from his sister.

Dear John,
I think that perhaps Olive's age has something to do with this problem. You have been married for ten years, and there have not been any children. At her age, her childbearing years are behind her, but it hasn't stopped her desire to be a mother. Have you considered adoption? Having a baby to love and care for might just snap her out of her melancholia. Give my love to Olive and tell her I'm praying for her.
Your sister,
Livinia

John re-read the letter several times. Of course, why hadn't he thought of it? He was so busy with his work and investments that he hadn't considered what Olive's life had become. She had her charity work, but that only amounted to a few hours a week. She had servants to do the housework and cooking, which left her with a great deal of free time on her hands. Her life, compared to his, was rather dreary and monotonous. Perhaps his sister was right.

That evening, after dinner, he broached the subject of adoption.

"But John, I thought you didn't care for children."

"Why do you think that, Olive? I simply haven't been around them that much. One is always a bit afraid of the unknown. I think I might make a better father than either of us suspect. What do you say?"

"Oh, John, I think it would be wonderful." For the first time in months, Olive smiled. Her face glowed with excitement.

On March 15, 1876, eleven years after their marriage, John and Olive Fairchild adopted a baby girl and named her Mary Elizabeth. However, they soon began calling her Mamie, and that name would become hers for the rest of her life. The change in Olive was miraculous. Mamie had given her a reason to live. John was happier too. He accepted the role of Papa with relish. He and Olive doted on little Mamie.

Although John and Olive attended St. Stephen's Episcopal Church, Mamie attended St. Joseph's Catholic Academy in Sherman.

Olive's health began to fail, and on August 2, 1881, John Fairchild wrote to Asa and Sarah Abbott, Olive's uncle and aunt in Illinois, informing them that Olive would be home by October 15th. He said she had been a patient at St. Catherine's Hospital in Ontario, Canada, where she had been confined to her bed most of the time.

St Catherine's was widely known for its mineral springs, steam baths, and curative waters. Unfortunately for Olive, the benefits were short lived and her illness progressed

On October 20, 1890, she wrote to her Aunt Sarah: "I am suffering with severe headache and cannot write more at this time."

On January 30, 1898, she wrote, with a shaky hand, to her Aunt Sarah: "I have been so very nervous, and my health has been very poor."

Olive's life was shattered when she learned of her Aunt Sarah's death on May 12, 1900. It was like losing her mother all over again. Then she learned of Lorenzo's death on October 8, 1901.

On March 20, 1903, Olive passed away at the age of sixty-five. She is buried in West Hill Cemetery in Sherman, Texas. John Fairchild died four years later.

Olive's neighbors would say, "She was a quiet, reserved, and gracious woman who always wore a veil in public to hide her tattoos."

Epilogue

Tribal records for the years 1850 to 1900 are mostly oral and therefore incomplete. A probable scenario follows.

Homeseh Awahot (Espaniole), great chief of the Mojaves, has one son, Cairook.

Cairook "marries" Olive Oatman in March of 1854. Their firstborn, in December of 1854, is named John (Empote Potachecha). Second-born is a son, name unknown, in November of 1855.

Olive is ransomed in February of 1856. Her youngest child is only two months old at the time.

Cairook remarries after Olive leaves. He accepts a temporary assignment as guide to a government survey team led by Lieutenant Joseph C. Ives in the winter of 1858.

In August 1858, the Rose-Baley wagon train is attacked on the Colorado by a large party of Mojaves.

On April 20, 1859, seven hundred soldiers, led by Colonel Hoffman, arrive at the Mojave village. Cairook and his two cousins are taken to Fort Yuma as hostages in retaliation for the attack on the Rose-Baley wagon train. Colonel Hoffman promises they will be released in one year.

On April 24, 1859, construction of Fort Mojave begins on the Colorado River to protect emigrants from the Mojave Indians. The fort is built in response to the attack upon the Rose-Baley wagon train.

A year later, April of 1860, Cairook and his cousins have not been released from the Fort Yuma prison. They attempt an escape, during which Cairook is killed.

About the same time, high-grade ores are discovered in the nearby Cerbat Mountains. Gold, silver, lead, zinc, and copper are mined there. These ores are sent around the horn (Cape Horn) to Wales for refining. The Mojaves cut wood for the riverboats and store it at strategic locations along the riverbank. Two powerful Mojaves are kept on board the riverboats. When a boat becomes mired in silt, two Mojaves leap into the water and, while one holds the plow handles, the other pulls the plow, creating a groove which increases the water flow and creates a new channel to deeper water.

When the riverboats return carrying salt and other items for the mining camps, the Mojaves unload them. One Mojave can carry a four-hundred-pound bag of salt on his back.

In 1861, due to constraints of the Civil War, the military abandon Fort Mojave. Espaniole is old, ill, and despondent over the death of his son, Cairook. He does not want the responsibility of great chief. His grandson, Empote Potachecha (John), is only six years old at the time his father, Cairook, is killed.

Yara Tav, Espaniole's brother, is named great chief to rule until Empote-John is old enough to assume the role.

In 1864, Yara Tav travels to Los Angeles, San Francisco, New York, and then to Washington, D.C., to meet with President Lincoln. He appeals to Lincoln to allow the Mojave to retain their tribal lands.

In March 1865, the United States government creates the Colorado Indian Reservation near Parker, Arizona. Even though this land is arid and unsuitable for agriculture, Yara Tav and about eight hundred Mojaves move to the new reservation in Parker Valley. Homeseh Awahot (Espaniole), now a very old man, resumes his role as great chief of the remaining tribe who refuse to leave the Mojave Valley. Thus the people were split into two tribes. Those living around the fort were called the Fort Mojave tribe.

In 1875, Olive's eldest son John (Empote Potachecha) becomes great chief at the age of twenty-one. He marries and has two sons, John Jr., born around 1878, and Hobelia, born in 1882. Great Chief Empote Potachecha (John) dies in 1890 at age thirty-six. Hobelia is eight years old at the time.

When the old fort building and fourteen thousand acres are transferred from the War Department to the Department of the Interior in 1890, the old fort becomes a boarding school for the Fort Mojave and other non-reservation Indian children. Attendance is compulsory and mandated by law.

The school is more like a prison than a school. Disobedience or truancy is severely punished by whipping and solitary confinement on a diet of bread and water. English is the only language to be spoken, and if a child unconsciously lapses into his native language, he is beaten. They are taught agricultural skills, which are useless as they do not own land. Many of these people find employment in the mines, on the Atlantic and Pacific Railroad (later named the Santa Fe), and on the riverboats.

Later, Mojave children are forced to abandon their tribal names and adopt English names. This leads to a great deal of confusion, as the children are allowed to select their English names from a list and those names are then applied to their parents as well. In some cases, two siblings choose different last names, adding to the confusion. If this isn't confusing enough, it is common practice among the Mojave to change their first names whenever they became tired of them.

Hobelia enters school in 1892 at the age of ten, and his name is Anglicized to Peter Lambert. When his older brother, John Jr., shows no inclination to become chief, Hobelia becomes eligible to assume the position. He will be the last of the great Mojave chiefs. Peter Lambert died in 1947, and the tribe now has a Tribal Council form of government.

John Jr. is more interested in gold mining. He leaves the tribe and relocates to Vivian, Arizona, where gold has been discovered. He calls himself John Oatman and claims to be the grandson of Olive Oatman. He begins panning for gold and becomes quite wealthy by local standards.

On June 24, 1909, at the instigation of mine owners James Knight and L. P. Hanson, the name of Vivian, Arizona, is officially changed to Oatman in honor of Olive, who had spent four years close by in the Mojave Valley. It was not named after John Oatman, despite rumors to that effect.

On April 30, 1922, an article entitled "Tribal Atrocities Alleged in Divorce Suit Against Wealthy Mojave Indian Outdoes Fiction" appeared in the (Phoenix) *Arizona Republican.* It reported:

> One of the most interesting legal battles in the history of Mojave County was fought out today in the Oatman Court of Domestic Relations when John Oatman, wealthy Mojave Indian, was sued for divorce by his wife, Estelle Oatman. Both plaintiff and defendant live near the Oatman gold camp in which the Mojave chief is heavily interested.
>
> John Oatman claims to be the grandson of Olive Oatman, famous in Arizona history.

The article goes on to describe, in great detail, all of the complaints of both parties to the action, some of which are so bizarre that they defy credulity among whites, but as they deal with the idiosyncrasies of tribal customs, would not shock the Mojaves.

In 1936, a great flood changes the course of the Colorado River, and it is estimated that the river, in the time Olive lived in the Mojave Valley, was approximately two miles from where it is today. In 1951, the Army Corps of Engineers cuts a straight channel on the Colorado from Topock, eleven miles long. Other cuts and dredging have taken place along the river, and many sloughs and marshlands have vanished, changing the landscape forever. All of the old dwellings in the Mojave village disappeared in the great flood.

What Became of ...?

Robert Kelly stayed on at Fort Yuma for a short time after his arrival with Lorenzo, the Wilders, and his brother, John. During that time, he was hired to build a boat out of whip-sawed cottonwood, the only trees available in that region. He left Fort Yuma long before Olive arrived and went on to Agua Hedrona, near San Diego, California, where he and his brother, John, owned and operated a ranch for a number of years before John left for northern California in 1860. There he met and married a woman named Catherine. They had a daughter named Anna Jane. John is buried in Vallejo, California.

Robert never responded to Olive's letter written from San Francisco on her way to the Rogue River Valley. Perhaps he had read the article in the *Los Angeles Star* in January of 1856 claiming that she was married to the chief's son and had two children. Or perhaps it was because her letter suggested that, as a result of her hardships, she had become depressed and morose, a completely different person from the one he had fallen in love with. Whatever his reasons, he never married, and it was said that "he carried his love for Olive in his heart, under a veil of silence, until his death." He died on November 12, 1890, at the age of sixty-five.

Reverend Royal B. Stratton wrote the first edition of *The Captivity of the Oatman Girls* when he was thirty years old. The book was published in San Francisco in 1857 and was a huge success. Stratton wrote a second edition with some additional anecdotes, which also sold out. This was followed by a third edition, published in New York.

To promote this last edition, he set up lecture tours for Olive and Lorenzo. He said his intent was to provide the means for an education for them. However, they had only attended classes in Santa Clara, California, for a few months before Stratton recruited them for a lecture tour in upstate New York to promote the book. They lived with Stratton in Albany, New York, where the lecture circuit kept them occupied.

However, Olive did attend grammar school in Albany for a short period of time before meeting and marrying John Fairchild in 1865.

In 1859, Stratton eliminated Lorenzo from the lecture circuit and retained Olive, the "star" of these presentations. Apparently, Lorenzo harbored no ill will toward the Rev. Stratton, because he named his only son Royal Fairchild Oatman. Royal was Stratton's first name, and his son's middle name was a tribute to John Fairchild, Olive's husband.

No one knows where all the proceeds from the three editions of the book went. The lectures were also profitable, even though a portion of the admission fees was donated to the churches in which the lectures were held. They always played to a packed house of curious patrons eager to see Olive's tattoos and hear her story in her own words. Olive's lecture notes have been preserved and are still available if one wishes to read them.

In July of 1860, Stratton became an "outdoor preacher" at Swan Street Methodist Church in Albany, New York. He later founded the Congregational Church of Albany.

It is interesting to note that, although Stratton was living in Albany at the time of Olive's marriage to John Fairchild on November 9, 1965, in Rochester, New York, he was not asked to perform the wedding ceremony, and in fact, was not invited to attend.

In 1865, after Olive's marriage to John Fairchild, Stratton moved to Worchester, Massachusetts, where he became pastor of the First Congregational Church. In the spring of 1867, he received word that his twenty-one-year-old son, Albert, had committed suicide in Santa Clara, California. This event, coupled with charges of erratic behavior by his parishioners, tended to send the Reverend Stratton into a deep depression. He was dismissed on April 25, 1872, due to mental illness. He died January 25, 1875, at the age of forty-eight, in an insane asylum. Cause of death was given as "disease of the brain." On the death register of Worchester, Massachusetts, cause of death is listed as "insanity."

Major Samuel P. Heintzelman, following his retirement from the U.S. Army, started the Sonora Mining and Exploring Company with Charles Poston in Cincinnati, Ohio, in 1856. The company was formed to mine copper. They later established headquarters in the abandoned *presidio* of Tubac, Arizona. They purchased the 17,000-acre ranch of Arivaca from Tomas and Ignacio Ortiz. The following spring, silver was discovered just north of Arivaca. Poston and Heintzelman's venture was touted as the "most important mining company on the continent."

The panic of 1857 caused the business to unravel. Heintzelman persuaded firearms inventor Samuel Colt to invest ten thousand dollars in the company. By 1859, Colt had seized control of the company.

Controversy Through the Years

Historians have had many different opinions regarding Olive's captivity. According to a letter written by Sharlot Hall, a noted historian, "Olive had two children while among her captors (Mojaves), and one of them sometimes visits Fort Yuma." This is an excerpt from the original letter in the Hayden file, Arizona Pioneer Historical Society. Sharlot Hall authored several articles about Olive Oatman. One of these, "Olive A. Oatman, Her Captivity With the Apache Indians and Her Later Life," appeared in *Out West* magazine on September 19, 1908.

Some, like Edward J. Pettid, a Catholic priest and historian, have maintained that "Olive's helplessness was respected by the Indians and that she was not violated or made a wife."

Others, such as historian Alford E. Turner, wrote:

> It should never be thought, however, that the life of a female captive of the Apaches was a bed of roses. It meant torture, hard work, famine, disease, and continuing sexual abuse. It was not unusual for an Indian to "rent" his slave to any man that wanted her, or for that matter, to any number of men in a single night.

Turner goes on to say:

> Two weeks after Olive's release from captivity, she and Lorenzo were interviewed by the *Los Angeles Star,* where their story was eagerly read by the public. The *Star* exhibited a first-class case of hypocrisy in denying that Olive had not been subjected to sexual abuse by the Indians.

The *Star* insisted,

> She had not suffered "a fate worse than death." She had not been made a wife. Her defenseless situation was entirely respected during her five-year residence among the Indians.

This article appeared in the *Star* as a correction to an earlier one stating that Olive had been married to an Indian and had two children.

Turner then says,

> If the *Star* was right in its contention that the Indians respected Olive's virginity for the five-year period of her slavery, she was, indeed, the first female captive to be so respected by Indians. The odds are even higher when we consider the Colorado River Indian tribes. The white society of 1856 simply could not face up to certain facts of life.

In the December 1958 issue of *True West Magazine,* there appeared an article by Freeman H. Hubbard entitled "Wife of the Chief." In it, he contends that Olive was married to Chief Espanesay (Espaniole), but other accounts contradict this, stating that she was married to Espaniole's son, Cairook.

One such account is the article written by Richard Dillon for the March/April 1981 issue of *American West Magazine* entitled "Tragedy at Oatman Flat: Massacre, Captivity, Mystery." In it, he quotes Susan Thompson, whose family traveled with the Oatmans on the wagon train and with whom Olive stayed for four months after leaving Fort Yuma. Susan flatly stated,

"Olive became the wife of the Mojave chief's son (Cairook), and she was the mother of two little boys at the time of her ransom."

Why would Susan lie? She was, after all, very close to the Oatman family. Olive did live with her for about four months after her release from captivity, and it was plausible that Olive confided in Susan in order to explain her depression at a time when she should have been elated. In writing this fictional account of a historical event and its aftermath, I have chosen to believe Susan. I leave it to the reader to draw his/her own conclusions.

DIRECTIONS TO MASSACRE SITE:

To reach the Oatman massacre site, the traveler should avoid crossing the Gila River. Take Interstate 8 to the Oatman Flats area. Several possible roads exist from the interstate, and it is difficult to say which is best. Upon reaching a wide place in the road called Sentinel, head north. Sentinel is thirty-three miles west of Gila Bend and ninety-five miles east of Yuma. Almost any trail north will take you to the south bank of the Gila River below (west of) Oatman Flats. There is a lava canyon leading from the flats to the Gila River. Along the south rim of the mesa is an old trail going east and west. Follow it to the cliffs overlooking the flats. Burke's Stage Station is off in the distance, and you should be at the Oatman massacre site. It is identified by a white pipe cross and a huge pile of lava rock. A four-wheel drive vehicle is recommended. Wear a hat, sunscreen, and sensible shoes, and bring lots of water. Morning is best, as afternoons can be hot. Don't attempt this during the summer months. A cell phone might come in handy in the event you become lost.

Bibliography

Arizona Highways Magazine, "The Oatman Story: Olive Oatman's Lecture Notes and Biography," November 1968.

Bancroft, Hubert Howe. *History of Arizona and New Mexico.* San Francisco, 1889, p. 485

Brown, Dee. *The Gentle Tamers,* pp.35 and 36, Bison Books, 1958.

Browne, John Ross. "A Tour Through Arizona," *Harpers Monthly,* November 1864.

Browne, John Ross. *Adventures in the Apache Country,*Chapter VII, pp. 87, 97, 98, New York, Harper and Brothers, 1869.

California Historical Society Quarterly, "Olive Ann Oatman: Lecture Notes and Biography," vol. XXI, pp. 107 through 112,1942.

Corle, Edwin. *The Gila.* New York: Reinhart & Co., 1951.

Dillon, Richard. "Tragedy at Oatman Flat: Massacre, Captivity, Mystery," *American West Magazine,* March/April 1981, pp 46-54, 59.

Dunn, Jacob P. Jr. *Massacres of the Mountains: A History of the Indian Wars of the Far West,1815–1875.*

Glassbrook, Trudy. "Death at Oatman Flat," *The Westerners,* vol. 16, no. 2, p. 37,1969.

H. D. Clark's Quest. *The Oatman Story.* pub. July 2002.

Hall, Sharlot M., "Olive Oatman: Her Captivity with the Apache Indians and Her Later Life," *Out West Magazine,* September 1908.

Holmes, Kenneth L., *Diaries of Covered Wagon Women,* Arthur H. Clark, Publishers, 1983.

Hubbard, Freeman H. "Wife of the Chief," *True West Magazine,* December 1958, p.16.

Hughes, Sam. "A Bit of History," *Arizona Enterprise,* 1890, 2 cols.

Ives, Lt. Joseph C. *Report Upon the Colorado River of the West, 1857-1858.* Army Corps of Engineers, Government Printing Office, 1861. Includes portrait of Yara Tav (Iretaba), Cairook, and Cairook's second wife with infant by Balduin Möllhausen.

Kelly Family Genealogy, posted on the internet August, 2007, p.4.

Kroeber, A. L. "Olive Oatman's Return." Let Us Reason Ministries, "Early History of the Mormon Church," vol. IV, 1951, online.

Los Angeles Star, "Arrival of Miss Oatman,". April 12, 1856, (Re: Olive's arrival in El Monte, California, at the home of the Ira Thompson family; full interview in *Star,* April 19, 1856.)

Maloney, Alice Bay. "Some Oatman Documents" from the Bancroft Library of the University of California, June 1942.

Michno, Gregory and Susan. *A Fate Worse Than Death.* pp. 87, 103-108, 462, 463, 473, Caxton Press, 1948.

Miller, Joseph. "The Arizona Story," *Tombstone Epitaph,* May 1982, p. 1 and pp. 6 through 9.

National Park Service, "Mojave Indians: History to Present," online.

Peckham, Howard H. *Captured by Indians,* 1954.

Phoenix, Arizona Republican, "Tribal Atrocities Alleged in Divorce: the Divorce of John Oatman, Wealthy Mojave Indian, and Wife, Estelle" April 30, 1922. (John Oatman claims to be Olive's grandson); Journal of Arizona History.

R. R. Donnelly & Son. *Vanished Arizona.* Lakeside Press.

Records of the Mohave Tribal Council. "Ki-e-chook: Marks Carried by All Married Mohave Women."

Root, Virginia V. *Following the Pot of Gold at the Rainbow's End in the Days of 1850: The Life of Mrs. Susan Thompson Lewis Parrish of El Monte, California,* from manuscript diary, Henry E Huntington Library, San Marino, California.

San Bernardino County Museum Association Quarterly, "Olive Oatman's Lecture Notes and Oatman Bibliography," winter 1968, vol. XVI, No. 2.

San Francisco Evening Bulletin, "Interview with Olive Oatman," June 24, 1856.

Schlissel, Lillian. *Women's Diaries of the Westward Journey,* p 872 to 978, Published by Schocken Books, 1987.

Sorensen, Cloyd Jr. "The Oatman Massacre Site," *True West Magazine,* March, 1984 p. 40, 41 and 42.

Spier, Leslie. *Yuman Tribes of the Gila River,* Dover Publications, 1978.

Stratton, R. B. *The Captivity of the Oatman Girls Among the Apache and Mohave Indians.* San Francisco: Grabhorn Press,1957.

Texas State Historical Society. "New Handbook of Texas Online." (Information on John and Olive Fairchild.)

Turner, Alford E., *Real West Magazine,* Spring 1983, pp. 16, 17.

Whipple, Lt. Amiel Weeks. *Reports of Explorations and Surveys to Ascertain the Most Practical and Economical Route for a Railroad from the Mississippi River to the Pacific Ocean.* Army Corps of Engineers, Government Printing Office, 1856.

Wikipedia, "Gadsden Purchase" and "Mexican-American War."

CPSIA information can be obtained at www.ICGtesting.com
Printed in the USA
LVOW080800130112

263431LV00001B/49/P